Manson: The Making of Madness

Written by

Darryl Harvey

Based on, True Events

INT. CORCORAN STATE PRISON - INTERVIEW ROOM - DAY

INSERT CARD: NOVEMBER 12, 1994, CALIFORNIA CORCORAN STATE PRISON

A grainy video with an obscure time code flickers on screen. The audio crackles with reverb. CHARLES MANSON, male white, 60, in a drab beige jumpsuit, sits shackled in a chair, his hair long and unkempt, a defiant look in his eyes.

                    CHARLES
              (leans forward, voice
               raspy)
          Not to hate you first. You're the
          first in line in my hate. I hate
          all white people. White people are
          rotten, and black people are just
          like 'em. Because you made 'em
          just exactly like you.

He pauses, his eyes scanning something—or someone—off-camera.

                    CHARLES (CONT'D)
          They wanna be you so much. They
          love your woman more than you do.
          They know your mind better than
          you. You strip 'em from their
          roots, put them in your mold.
          Isn't that so?

Manson's voice grows louder, more intense.

                    CHARLES (CONT'D)
          You take 'em out of the jungle and
          wanna make 'em into a man. Why
          couldn't it be left up to GOD, huh?
          In the jungle, they were GOD.
          Africans are smart, aren't they?
          Over here, everybody thinks they're
          just old dumb colored folk. But
          they're not. They're very smart,
          very aware. And their capacity for
          fear? It's three times what yours
          is.

His laugh is bitter, echoing around the small room as he leans back, the chains clinking softly.

                    CHARLES (CONT'D)
          Yeah, they learn fast. Too fast
          for you, maybe. That scares you,
          doesn't it?

The camera zooms out slowly, leaving Manson's piercing gaze as the last image before the screen fades to black.

INT. UNIVERSITY OF CINCINNATI ACADEMIC HEALTH CENTER - DELIVERY ROOM - DAY (1934)

The room is sparse, the air tense. ADA KATHLEEN MADDOX, female white, 15, lies exhausted on the hospital bed, clutching a newborn. The baby cries faintly as the NURSE stands by.

                    NURSE
               (softly)
          What will you name him, dear?

Ada looks down at the baby with a mix of fear and affection.

                    ADA
          Charles. Charles Milles Maddox.

The nurse smiles, making notes. Ada's expression shifts, reflecting deeper concerns.

                    ADA (CONT'D) (CONT'D)
          His father... he said he was a
          colonel, had to leave for army
          business. I thought he'd come to
          see his son.

Her voice trails off, filled with doubt and a touch of bitterness.

                    NURSE
               (reassuringly)
          You're both going to be just fine.
          Do you have someone to help you at
          home?

Ada nods weakly, her mind elsewhere, pondering the reality of raising Charles alone.

                    ADA
          Yes, my mother... but I really
          thought he'd be here.

The nurse pats Ada's hand gently, understanding the gravity of her solitude.

                    NURSE
          He's beautiful, Ada. He's got your
          strength already.

Ada forces a smile, her eyes on Charles, filled with
uncertain hopes and dreams for her son's future.

INT. TAVERN - NIGHT (1937)

The setting is dimly lit and smoke-filled. Ada Kathleen
Maddox, now 18, sits with her brother, LUTHER ELBERT MADDOX,
male white, 21, each with a drink in hand. Their
conversation is heated, with undertones of frustration and
resignation.

> LUTHER
> (to Ada, concerned)
> You're spiraling, Ada. This ain't
> good for you or the boy.

Ada rolls her eyes, taking a long sip of her drink.

> ADA
> Charles will be fine. The sitters
> are good with him. I need this
> time, Luther.

> LUTHER
> (sighing)
> You think William doesn't see
> what's happening? He's a good man,
> Ada.

> ADA
> (defensively)
> A good man? That 'good man' barely
> looks at his own stepson. What's
> he care if I find some happiness?

Luther leans in, voice lowering.

> LUTHER
> He's talking divorce, Ada. Saying
> you're neglecting your duties.

Ada laughs bitterly, shakes her head.

> ADA
> Let him try. Charles will always
> be a Maddox, no matter what name he
> carries.

Luther watches his sister, worry etching deeper into his
features.

                         LUTHER
          And what about when we're not here
          to pick up the pieces? You gonna
          leave him all alone then?

Ada's façade cracks, a moment of vulnerability showing
through.

                         ADA
               (fiercely)
          Never. We'll figure this out, just
          like we always do.

The siblings clink glasses, a pact between them as they dive
back into the noise of the tavern, leaving the future
uncertain.

INT. POLICE STATION - INTERROGATION ROOM - DAY (1939)

Ada Kathleen Maddox, now 20, sits across from a DETECTIVE,
her demeanor defiant yet anxious. Luther Elbert Maddox, now
23, is visible through the glass, in a separate room, looking
resigned.

                         DETECTIVE
               (pointing to documents)
          Assault and robbery, Ada. This is
          serious. Why'd you do it?

Ada glares, her voice sharp.

                         ADA
          We needed the money. Wasn't
          planning to hurt nobody.

                         DETECTIVE
               (skeptically)
          Your brother's got a different
          story. Says it was your idea.

Ada's eyes flicker towards the glass, seeing Luther, then
back to the Detective.

                         ADA
               (firmly)
          Luther would say the moon is made
          of cheese if you asked him right.
          We stick together.

The Detective leans back, assessing her.

>   DETECTIVE
>   He's looking at ten years, you at
>   five. That sticking together might
>   cost you more than you bargained
>   for.

Ada's façade slightly cracks, revealing fear.

>   ADA
>   (softly)
>   What about my boy? What happens to
>   Charles?

>   DETECTIVE
>   He'll be put in foster care.
>   Unless you got family can take him?

Ada shakes her head, a tear escaping.

>   ADA
>   No. Just us.

The Detective notes her reaction, his tone softening a bit.

>   DETECTIVE
>   I can try to push for a lighter
>   sentence. But I need the whole
>   story, Ada. Everything.

Ada looks towards Luther again, tears now freely flowing,
then nods slowly, ready to bargain for her son's future.

EXT. THOMAS FAMILY HOME - BACKYARD - DAY

The yard is quiet, save for the rustle of leaves. JO ANN
THOMAS, female, 10, anxiously watches CHARLES MANSON, 7,
mischievous and defiant, as he plays.

>   JO ANN
>   I have to go inside and change the
>   bed linens.
>   (goading)
>   Charlie, don't wander off too far,
>   okay? Stay where I can see you.

Charles ignores her, digging through a pile of old tools and
pulls out a shiny sickle. His eyes light up with a troubling
gleam. He runs back towards the house, sickle in hand.

>   CHARLES
>   (elated, waving the
>   sickle)
>   Look what I found!

Jo Ann, alarmed, tries to snatch the sickle but Charles
dodges, waving it more aggressively.

                    JO ANN
               (terrified, shouting)
          Charlie, stop! You're going to
          hurt someone!

Charles continues slashing at the air until Jo Ann, in a
quick move, locks the screen door between them. Charles face
twists in anger as he starts slashing at the screen door.

                    JO ANN (CONT'D)
               (inside, yelling through
                the door)
          Stop it, Charlie! You're scaring
          me!

Charles, undeterred, rips through the screen, his expression
wild. Just then, BILL and GLENNA THOMAS pull into the
driveway. They rush out of the car, shocked at the scene.

                    BILL
               (stern, approaching)
          Charlie! What in God's name are
          you doing?

Jo Ann, near tears, points at Charles, too scared to speak.

                    JO ANN
               (barely audible)
          Ask Charlie...

Charles, still holding the sickle, looks defiantly at his
uncle.

                    CHARLES
               (defensively)
          She attacked me first! I was just
          protecting myself!

Bill takes the sickle from Charles and grabs his arm,
dragging him towards the house.

                    BILL
               (firmly)
          Enough of this nonsense! You're
          getting a whipping for this, young
          man!

Bill leads Charles away for his punishment, while Glenna
comforts a shaken Jo Ann, throwing a worried glance back at
Charles.

                    GLENNA
              (softly, to Jo Ann)
         It's okay, honey. We're here now.

Bill disappears into the house with Charles, the sounds of
discipline echoing faintly.

FLASHBACK:

INT. SMALL TOWN HOME - KITCHEN - DAY (1934)

In a modest, sunlit kitchen where Ada Maddox, 15, nervously
prepares tea. The air is heavy with anticipation and
anxiety. Her hands tremble slightly as she pours the hot
water.

                    ADA
              (whispering to herself)
         This can't be real.

The door creaks open, and WILLIAM EUGENE MANSON, male white,
25, steps in. He's a rugged man, his clothes slightly worn
from labor, but his eyes are kind and searching.

                    WILLIAM
              (softly)
         Ada, you sure about this?

Ada turns, her face pale but resolute.

                    ADA
              (starting to sit, then
               standing again)
         I... We need to do this, William.
         It's the only way.

William nods, understanding the weight of the moment. He
steps closer, taking her hands in his.

                    WILLIAM
              (gently)
         If this is what you want, I'm here.
         We'll raise him right, together.

Ada nods, tears welling up as she looks up into William's
reassuring face.

                    ADA
              (thankful)
         Thank you, William. I... I don't
         know what I'd do without you.

Ada and William share a quiet, supportive embrace, setting a tone of makeshift family against all odds.

INT. LOCAL BAR - NIGHT

The camera cuts to a darker scene, where Luther Elbert Maddox, Ada's brother, lifts a glass in a dimly lit bar. Ada sits beside him, her expression distant.

> LUTHER
> (raising his glass)
> To new beginnings, eh?

Ada forces a smile, sipping her drink. The night progresses with laughter and too many drinks. The bar fades into the background as Ada's thoughts drift to her unborn child.

INT. MANSON HOUSEHOLD - LIVING ROOM - DAY (1937)

Three years later, the strain is visible. Papers are strewn about a table. Ada and William stand opposite each other, voices raised but weary.

> WILLIAM
> (angry and frustrated)
> You're never here, Ada! I'm
> trying, but I can't do this alone!

Ada, her spirit fading, slumps into a chair, defeated.

> ADA
> (pleading)
> I don't know how to be what you
> need. I'm trying, too, William.

William softens, the anger giving way to sorrow.

> WILLIAM
> (softly)
> I wanted us to be a family, Ada.
> For Charlie's sake.

Ada looks away, guilt-ridden. A beat of silence passes.

> ADA
> (quietly)
> I wanted that too.

INT. COURTHOUSE - DAY

The courtroom is nearly empty, the echoes of finality
lingering in the air. Ada Kathleen Maddox Manson, visibly
aged beyond her years, stands at a table, signing the last of
the divorce papers. Across from her, William Manson watches,
his expression a mixture of relief and sorrow.

>   ADA
>   (voice trembling)
>   Is this it then?

>   WILLIAM
>   (resignedly)
>   It's for the best, Ada. For both
>   of us.

Ada sets down the pen, her hands shaking slightly. She looks
up at William, her eyes searching for something long lost.

>   ADA
>   (softly)
>   I never wanted it to end like this.

>   WILLIAM
>   (sighs deeply)
>   Neither did I, Ada. Neither did I.

Ada picks up the finalized papers, her grip tightening around
them.

>   ADA
>   (whispers to herself as
>   she turns to leave)
>   For Charlie...

She walks away, each step heavy, leaving William standing
alone, watching her go with a look of profound sadness.

EXT. COURTHOUSE - MOMENTS LATER

Ada steps into the daylight, her face set against the pain,
determined to forge ahead despite the odds.

EXT. PLAYGROUND - DAY

Young CHARLES MANSON, now three-years-old, plays under the
watchful eye of a babysitter. He is oblivious to the
complexities that led to his fractured family life.

Ada watching from a distance, her face a mix of love and regret. She turns and walks away, leaving a piece of her heart behind with her young son.

END FLASHBACK.

INT. SMALL APARTMENT - LIVING ROOM - DAY (1942)

A modest living room is bathed in the warm glow of afternoon sunlight. CHARLES MANSON, 8, excitedly arranges a small welcome home banner across the mantelpiece. The sound of a key turning in the lock causes him to turn, his face lighting up with joy.

Ada, now 23, steps through the door, her appearance weary yet softened by the sight of her son. She drops her bag and opens her arms as Charles rushes into her embrace.

                    ADA
               (voice cracking with
                emotion)
          Oh, Charlie, I've missed you so
          much.

Charles, muffled against his mother's chest, speaks with innocent enthusiasm.

                    CHARLES
          I made this banner for you, Mama.
          Do you like it?

Ada pulls back, tears in her eyes, nodding as she takes in the crude yet heartfelt decoration.

                    ADA
               (smiling through tears)
          I love it, Charlie. It's perfect.

The room fills with laughter and soft chatter as Ada and Charles sit down on the sofa, Charles excitedly recounting tales of his life without her.

                    CHARLES
               (rambling with excitement)
          And then Mr. Jenkins let me help at
          the store, and I got to put the
          cans on the shelf just like a grown-
          up!

                    ADA
               (amused and proud)
          Is that so? My little man working
          already?

Charles nods vigorously, basking in his mother's attention.

> CHARLES
> Yeah, and I saved all the nickels
> he gave me in the jar! We can buy
> bread and jam.

Ada's eyes glisten with mixed emotions, proud of her son's resilience yet saddened by the necessity of his maturity at such a young age.

> ADA
> (reassuringly)
> You're amazing, Charlie. But now,
> I'm home. We'll do things
> together, okay?

Charles face beams as he leans against her, feeling secure and loved.

> CHARLES
> Promise, Mama?

> ADA
> (softly, kissing his
> forehead)
> Promise.

They spend the evening playing simple games and sharing a modest dinner, reveling in their reunion. The apartment, small and unassuming, is filled with laughter and stories, marking the beginning of a brief, cherished chapter in Charles childhood.

INT. MANSON APARTMENT - CHARLESTON, WEST VIRGINIA - EVENING

Now in a dimly lit, cluttered apartment in Charleston, revealing Charles Manson, 8 years old, slipping out the front door with a mischievous grin. Ada, 23, is seen pouring herself a drink in the kitchen, her expression weary and distant.

EXT. CHARLESTON STREETS - LATE AFTERNOON

Charles wanders the streets, joining a group of older kids in a vacant lot. They're skipping stones and sharing tales of minor mischief. Charles, eager to fit in, listens intently, absorbing every word as the sun begins to set.

                    CHARLES
               (excitedly)
          You guys really sneak into the
          movie theater through the back?

One of the older boys, TOM, male white, 12, nods with a sly
smile.

                    TOM
               (grinning)
          Every Saturday. You should come
          with us next time, runt.

Charles beams at the invitation, feeling a sense of belonging
he seldom feels at home.

INT. MANSON APARTMENT - NIGHT

Ada is slumped at the table, surrounded by empty bottles.
The room is dim, save for the flicker of a television screen.

The sound of the front door creaking open catches Ada's
attention. She turns to see Charles sneaking in. Her voice
is slurred but stern.

                    ADA
               (annoyed)
          Where have you been, Charlie? It's
          past your bedtime!

                    CHARLES
               (defensively)
          Just out playing, Ma. Everyone
          stays out late here.

Ada sighs, the fight draining from her. She gestures vaguely
toward his room.

                    ADA
               (tiredly)
          Just go to bed, Charlie. We'll
          talk tomorrow.

Charles nods, escaping to his room while Ada turns back to
her drink, her solitude enveloping her once more.

INT. CHARLES BEDROOM - NIGHT

Charles lies in bed, staring at the ceiling. The sounds of
distant laughter from the street mingle with the low murmur
of the TV from the next room.

He clutches a small stone from his pocket, a token from his adventures, a small comfort against the loneliness of his home life.

INT. POLICE STATION - INTERROGATION ROOM - NIGHT

The room is stark and coldly lit. Ada, now visibly aged and stressed, sits across from DETECTIVE JONES, male white, 40, a seasoned officer with a stern demeanor. Papers and photos are spread out on the table between them.

                    DETECTIVE JONES
               (looking directly at Ada)
          Ms. Maddox, you were found in
          possession of items reported stolen
          from the downtown department store.
          How do you explain that?

Ada shifts uncomfortably in her chair, her hands trembling slightly but her voice is steady.

                    ADA
               (earnestly)
          I found those items, Detective.
          Near the alley by Halson Street. I
          didn't steal anything.

                    DETECTIVE JONES
               (skeptically)
          You "found" brand new items still
          with their tags on, dumped in an
          alley?

Ada nods, desperation creeping into her expression.

                    ADA
          Yes, I swear it! I was just there
          at the wrong time. I thought it
          was abandoned, maybe thrown out. I
          didn't think...

The detective leans back, not convinced, as he taps on the photographs showing the stolen goods recovered from Ada's home.

                    DETECTIVE JONES
               (firmly)
          Ms. Maddox, your story is hard to
          believe. You need to come clean if
          you want any chance at leniency.

Ada's eyes fill with tears, her fear palpable.

                    ADA
               (pleading)
          Please, Detective. I'm telling the
          truth. I can't go back to
          prison—I've got a son to take care
          of.

The detective sighs, his expression softening slightly as he
considers her plea.

                    DETECTIVE JONES
               (after a pause)
          I'll review the evidence again, but
          I need more than just your word,
          Ada.

INT. COURTROOM - DAY

Ada sits nervously as her lawyer, MR. EDWARDS, male white,
50, a competent but weary-looking man, addresses the judge.

The courtroom is filled with the low murmur of the audience.

                    MR. EDWARDS
               (confidently)
          Your Honor, the prosecution has not
          met the burden of proof required
          for grand larceny. My client found
          these items, as she has
          consistently stated.

The JUDGE, an older white man, 50s, with a thoughtful look,
nods as he listens, jotting down notes.

                    JUDGE
               (turning to the
                prosecutor)
          Does the prosecution have any
          witnesses or further evidence
          linking Ms. Maddox directly to the
          scene of the crime?

The PROSECUTOR, male white, 40, clearly flustered, shuffles
papers but finds nothing conclusive.

                    PROSECUTOR
               (reluctantly)
          No, Your Honor. We rely on the
          circumstantial evidence provided.

The judge takes a moment, then speaks with authority.

                    JUDGE
               (determined)
          Given the lack of direct evidence
          and the defendant's consistent
          account of how she came into
          possession of the items, I find the
          evidence insufficient for a
          conviction. The case against Ada
          Maddox is dismissed.

Ada's relief is overwhelming as she breaks down in tears.
Mr. Edwards pats her back reassuringly.

                    ADA
               (whispering, tearful)
          Thank you.

INT. ALCOHOLICS ANONYMOUS MEETING ROOM - INDIANAPOLIS -
EVENING (1943)

The room is modest, chairs arranged in a circle. Ada Maddox,
looking worn but hopeful, sits nervously among the group.
Across from her, LEWIS WOODSON CAVENDER JR., male white, 27,
an alcoholic trying to find his footing, shares his
struggles. Their eyes meet occasionally, a spark of mutual
understanding glinting between them.

                    LEWIS
               (earnestly, concluding his
                share)
          ...and every day is a battle, but
          I'm still here, still fighting.
          Thank you for listening.

The group murmurs their support as Lewis catches Ada's eye,
offering a shy smile.

                    ADA
               (encouragingly, when it's
                her turn)
          Thank you, Lewis. It's... it's my
          first time here. I'm Ada. I'm not
          the one with the drinking problem,
          but I've been around it my whole
          life. My husband, my brother...
          it's like this shadow that's always
          looming, you know?

The group nods empathetically as Ada continues, her voice a
mixture of strength and vulnerability.

                    ADA (CONT'D)
               (continuing)
          I guess I'm just trying to
          understand, to help where I can.
          Maybe make things different this
          time.

As the meeting concludes, people start to shuffle out. Lewis
approaches Ada, hesitantly at first.

                    LEWIS
               (gently)
          Ada, right? I couldn't help but
          feel like you were talking right to
          me. Maybe... maybe we could talk
          some more? Maybe help each other?

Ada looks at him, a cautious hope rising within her.

                    ADA
               (smiling slightly)
          I'd like that, Lewis. I really
          would.

They exchange numbers, a small yet significant step. As they
leave the building, there's a sense of new beginnings in the
air, the night somehow feeling a bit lighter.

EXT. INDIANAPOLIS STREET - NIGHT

Ada and Lewis walk together under the streetlights, their
conversation easy and relaxed. Ada glances around the new
cityscape with a mix of apprehension and hope.

                    ADA
               (smiling, with a hint of
                nervousness)
          It's a fresh start for us here,
          Lewis. My son and I just moved to
          Indianapolis. I'm hoping it'll be
          good for him... for both of us.

Lewis nods understandingly, offering a supportive smile as
they continue walking, their steps in sync. The image of two
people, once strangers bound by their struggles, now walking
side by side toward a hopeful future.

INT. ELEMENTARY SCHOOL - HALLWAY - DAY

The school is bustling with children transitioning between
classes. CHARLES MANSON, 9, mischievous and restless, sneaks
away from the crowd, a box of matches in his hand.

He peers around the corner to make sure no one is watching, then slips into the janitor's closet.

INT. JANITOR'S CLOSET - DAY

Charles flicks a match, watching it glow. The flame reflects in his eyes, a mix of fascination and defiance. He lights a small pile of papers and rags tucked in a corner. The fire catches quickly, growing brighter.

                    CHARLES
               (whispering to himself)
          That'll show them.

He slips out, leaving the door slightly ajar, the fire crackling behind him.

EXT. SCHOOL PLAYGROUND - DAY

Later, as fire trucks wail in the distance, Charles blends into a group of students gathered outside, watching as smoke billows into the sky.

Teachers rush to account for all the students, their faces marked with concern and fear.

                    TEACHER
               (frantic)
          Everyone, stay together! We need
          to make sure all students are
          accounted for.

Charles watches, a small smirk playing on his lips, unnoticed in the chaos.

INT. PRINCIPAL'S OFFICE - DAY - LATER

The principal, MR. HARRISON, male white, 42, a stern man, sits across from Charles, who appears indifferent. The smell of smoke still lingers on his clothes.

                    MR. HARRISON
               (sternly)
          Charles, this isn't just about
          skipping classes or stealing from
          the cafeteria. Setting a fire is
          serious. You could have hurt
          someone.

Charles shrugs, his gaze defiant.

> CHARLES
> (brazenly)
> I didn't mean to hurt anyone. I
> just wanted some excitement.

Mr. Harrison sighs deeply, realizing the gravity of Charles
troubled behavior.

> MR. HARRISON
> (concerned)
> We're going to have to call your
> mother, and there will be
> consequences for this, Charles.
> This can't go on.

Charles slouches, his façade of toughness waning slightly as
the reality of the situation sets in.

EXT. GIBAULT SCHOOL FOR BOYS - TERRE HAUTE, INDIANA - DAY

INSERT CARD: 1947

The imposing façade of the Gibault School for Boys looms
under a gray sky.

Young CHARLES MANSON, 13, stands in front of the tall, iron
gates, clutching a small bag of belongings, his expression a
mix of apprehension and defiance.

INT. GIBAULT SCHOOL FOR BOYS - HALLWAY - DAY

The hallways are stark, lined with stern portraits of past
educators. Manson is led by a strict-looking PRIEST, his
steps echoing loudly. They stop in front of a heavy wooden
door.

> PRIEST
> (firmly)
> This is your new home, Charles.
> Remember, we have rules here.
> Rules that are strictly enforced.

Manson nods, eyes darting around, taking in the strict,
disciplined atmosphere.

INT. GIBAULT SCHOOL FOR BOYS - DORMITORY - DAY

Manson is introduced to a spartan room with several beds.
The other boys give him a cautious look, sizing him up. One
of the boys, BOB, male white, 13, leans over from the
adjacent bed.

                         BOB
                    (whispering)
               Watch yourself here. The priests
               don't mess around. Step out of
               line, and it's the paddle or strap
               for you.

Manson absorbs this, his face hardening as he unpacks his few
belongings.

INT. GIBAULT SCHOOL FOR BOYS - CLASSROOM - DAY

The classroom is rigid, boys in neat rows. Manson struggles
to concentrate, fidgeting under the watchful eyes of another
stern PRIEST. A small mistake on his assignment leads to a
sharp reprimand.

                         PRIEST #2
                    (sharply)
               Manson! Pay attention! Do it
               again, correctly this time.

Manson nods, frustration simmering as he erases his work, the
room suffocatingly silent except for the scrape of his
pencil.

INT. GIBAULT SCHOOL FOR BOYS - CHAPEL - DAY

The boys are lined up for morning prayers. Manson stands
among them, the recitations echoing off the chapel walls.
His expression is distant, his mind wandering away from the
verses of penance and obedience.

INT. GIBAULT SCHOOL FOR BOYS - HEADMASTER'S OFFICE - DAY

After a minor infraction, Manson is brought before the
HEADMASTER, a priest with a reputation for strict discipline.
The sound of a wooden paddle being handled ominously fills
the tense air.

                         HEADMASTER
                    (gravely)
               Charles, you know the rules.
               Disobedience cannot be tolerated.

The Headmaster's words are stern as he picks up the leather
strap, Manson's face sets, bracing for the inevitable
punishment.

EXT. WOODS NEAR TERRE HAUTE - NIGHT

The moon casts ghostly shadows through the dense Indiana
woods. Charles Manson, 13, runs breathlessly, his escape
from the Gibault School for Boys marked by desperation.
Exhausted, he collapses under a large oak tree, his breath
visible in the cold night air.

                    CHARLES
               (whispering to himself)
          Can't go back... can't.

He curls up, using his thin jacket as a blanket, the sounds
of the forest both frightening and oddly comforting compared
to the stern discipline of Gibault.

EXT. UNDER A BRIDGE - DAY

The next morning, Manson finds himself under a bridge. Other
vagrants are scattered around, remnants of small fires
dotting the area. He approaches an older man, FRANK, male
Black 50s, who is warming his hands by a dying fire.

                    CHARLES
               (tentatively)
          Got any food?

                    FRANK
               (gruffly)
          Might share for some work. Help me
          gather more wood.

Charles nods, eager for any warmth and sustenance. He spends
the day collecting wood, earning not only food but also a
crash course in surviving on the streets.

EXT. CITY PARK - EVENING

As days turn into weeks, Manson learns to navigate urban
survival. In a city park, he huddles in a makeshift shelter
made from newspapers and cardboard. He watches families pass
by, a pang of longing mixed with growing resentment stirring
within him.

                    CHARLES
               (muttering to himself)
          They don't know how good they got
          it.

His gaze hardens as he pulls the cardboard closer, shielding
himself from the cold wind that sweeps through the park.

EXT. ALLEYWAY - NIGHT

Finding refuge in an alleyway lined with dumpsters, Manson
scavenges for food. He's dirty, his clothes ragged, but his
eyes have adapted to the harshness of his life. He's quick,
stealthy, and growing more adept at living in the shadows.

                    CHARLES
               (to himself, rummaging
                through trash)
          Finders keepers...

He uncovers a half-eaten sandwich, his small victory in the
relentless struggle of his daily existence.

EXT. RAILROAD TRACKS - DAY

Manson eventually finds solace in the transient community
along the railroad tracks. Surrounded by other runaways and
hobos, he listens intently to their stories, learning the
rhythms of a life on the move an OLD HOBO.

                    OLD HOBO
               (laughing, sharing wisdom)
          You gotta be like the river, boy.
          Keep moving, or you'll freeze up.

Manson nods, absorbing every word, his resolve to never
return to Gibault—or anyplace like it—cementing with each
passing day.

EXT. THOMAS FAMILY HOME - WEST VIRGINIA - DAY

INSERT CARD: CHRISTMAS 1947

Snow blankets the quaint Thomas family home in West Virginia.
Charles Manson, now a troubled 13-year-old, hesitantly
approaches the warmly lit house, his breath visible in the
cold air. The door opens to reveal his Aunt Glenna, who
greets him with a cautious but warm smile.

                    GLENNA
               (softly)
          Welcome home, Charlie. Come in,
          it's cold out there.

Charles steps inside, the warmth of the house enveloping him.
The sounds of Christmas carols and the scent of pine fill the
air.

INT. THOMAS FAMILY HOME - LIVING ROOM - NIGHT

The room is decorated with festive ornaments and a brightly lit Christmas tree.

Bill, a stern but fair man, nods at Charles, inviting him to join the family gathering.

                    BILL
               (gruffly)
          Sit down, boy. Join us.

Charles sits awkwardly on the edge of a couch, watching his cousin Jo Ann open presents. There's a palpable sense of belonging that he yearns for but feels just out of reach.

LATER THAT NIGHT

Charles lies in a small guest room, staring at the ceiling, reflecting on the temporary respite from his troubled life. His thoughts are interrupted as 28-year-old Ada, his mother, enters the room.

                    ADA
               (quietly)
          Charlie, we need to talk about you
          going back to Gibault.

Charles sits up, his expression a mix of fear and defiance.

                    CHARLES
               (pleading)
          Mom, please. I can't go back
          there. It's... it's horrible.

                    ADA
               (resolute)
          It's for the best, Charlie. You
          need structure, and I can't provide
          that for you right now.

Charles looks away, tears forming. He feels betrayed but powerless.

EXT. THOMAS FAMILY HOME - DAY

INSERT CARD: TEN MONTHS LATER

In a blur of discontent and rebellion for Charles. One brisk morning, he makes a decision. With a small bag slung over his shoulder, he leaves the Thomas home at dawn, not looking back.

INT. BUS STATION - DAY

Charles purchases a ticket with the last of his money. His
destination: Indianapolis. As the bus pulls away, he watches
the familiar landscapes of West Virginia fade into the
distance, his heart set on a new beginning—or at least an
escape from his past.

EXT. INDIANAPOLIS - DAY

The bus arrives in a bustling Indianapolis. Charles steps
off, overwhelmed but determined. The city noises, the
crowd—it's all daunting yet thrilling. He's on his own now,
truly on his own, in the vast urban landscape.

EXT. GROCERY STORE - INDIANAPOLIS - NIGHT

INSERT CARD: 1948

Under the cover of darkness, a young Charles Manson, looking
gaunt and desperate, lurks outside a small grocery store.
His eyes dart around, ensuring no one is watching, before he
picks the lock and slips inside.

INT. GROCERY STORE - CONTINUOUS

Manson moves quickly through the aisles, grabbing a loaf of
bread and some cheese. His movements are frantic, fueled by
hunger. As he stuffs the food into a worn bag, his hand
knocks over a cigar box hidden under the counter. The box
falls open, revealing a stack of cash—just over a hundred
dollars.

                    CHARLES
               (whispering to himself)
          Oh, man...

His initial shock gives way to a calculating look. He grabs
the money, his survival instinct overtaking any residual
hesitation.

I/E. SKID ROW - DINGY BUILDING - DAY

Manson, now flush with cash, walks confidently down Skid Row.
He enters a dingy building, negotiating with a skeptical
LANDLORD for a room.

                    LANDLORD
               (doubtfully)
          You got enough for a week?

                         CHARLES
                 (grinning, pulling out the
                 cash)
           I got enough. Keep the change.

The landlord eyes the money and nods, handing over the keys.

INT. MANSON'S RENTED ROOM - DAY

The room is stark, a bare bulb casting shadows on the faded
wallpaper. Charles Manson, carrying a couple of worn grocery
bags, steps inside. The room features just the essentials—a
small bed, a rickety chair, and a wooden table.

Manson sets the groceries on the table, carefully unpacking
each item: bread, some cheese, canned goods. He sits on the
edge of the bed, pulls out the wad of cash from his pocket,
and starts to count it meticulously.

                         CHARLES
                 (muttering to himself as
                 he arranges the food)
           This should last me a while.

He looks around the room, his gaze settling on the modest
stash of food. A sense of grim satisfaction washes over him.
For the first time in what feels like forever, Manson
experiences a semblance of stability and control, even though
it's built on shaky ground.

EXT. STREETS OF INDIANAPOLIS - DAY (

Charles Manson, 15, in a Western Union uniform, darts
energetically between buildings, delivering messages. His
face shows fleeting satisfaction in his honest work, yet
hints of underlying restlessness.

INT. WESTERN UNION OFFICE - DAY

Manson receives his paycheck, his face crumpling in
frustration at the meager amount.

                         CHARLES
                 (mutters to himself)
           This won't get me anywhere.

Spotting an unattended wallet, he swiftly pockets it with a
practiced glance around.

EXT. INDIANAPOLIS STREET - LATER

Manson's confidence grows as he stealthily lifts an apple
from a street vendor. His excitement is palpable, mixed with
a dangerous thrill.

INT. COURTROOM - DAY

Manson stands before a JUDGE, male white, 40, caught and
resigned, the judge looks at him with a blend of sternness
and sympathy.

                    JUDGE
               (somberly)
          Charles, I'm sending you to Boys
          Town. It's a chance for a fresh
          start... Make it count.

                    CHARLES
               (quietly)
          Yes, sir.

EXT. BOYS TOWN, OMAHA, NEBRASKA - DAY

Days later, Manson whispers to his fellow student, BLACKIE
NIELSON, male white, 15. Their faces are set with
determination.

                    CHARLES
               (whispering)
          We can't stay here, Blackie. We
          gotta get out.

In the parking lot, they steal a car in a rush of adrenaline
and fear.

EXT. RURAL ROAD - NIGHT

Manson and Blackie, fueled by adrenaline and the thrill of
their newfound freedom, target a solitary driver stopped to
change a flat tire.

Manson approaches cautiously, gun in hand, while Blackie
keeps watch. The driver, a middle-aged man, complies in
fear, handing over his wallet and watch.

                    CHARLES
               (hushed, urgent)
          Just keep calm, do what we say, and
          you won't get hurt.

As they flee with their meager loot, the boys spot a small
gas station, dimly lit and seemingly unprotected. They rush
in, faces covered with makeshift masks. The attendant, a
young woman, is too shocked to react as they empty the
register.

                    BLACKIE
              (excited, clutching the
              stolen cash)
         This is real freedom, Charlie!

They escape into the night, the sounds of sirens in the
distance growing fainter as they drive away, deeper into the
darkness of the rural landscape.

EXT. PEORIA, ILLINOIS - NIGHT

Arriving at NIELSON'S UNCLE'S house, male white, 30s. The
boys are greeted with a nod of approval and a wry smile.

                    NIELSON'S UNCLE
              (grinning)
         Looks like you boys could use a
         mentor. Let's see what you're made
         of.

INT. PEORIA STORE - NIGHT

INSERT CARD: TWO WEEKS LATER

During a store raid, police lights flash suddenly. Manson is
cuffed, his earlier confidence shattered by the reality of
his capture.

INT. POLICE STATION - INTERROGATION ROOM - NIGHT

Manson, under harsh interrogation lights, links himself to
prior crimes, his defiance fading into resignation.

INT. JUDGE'S CHAMBER - DAY

The sympathetic Judge now looks on with disappointment.

                    JUDGE
              (shaking his head)
         I hoped for better, Charles. I'm
         left with no choice but to send you
         to the Indiana Boys School. It's
         strict, but maybe that's what you
         need.

Manson, head bowed, accepts his fate, the weight of his decisions settling heavily on his young shoulders.

INT. INDIANA BOYS SCHOOL - DORMITORY - NIGHT

The stark, dimly-lit dormitory at the Indiana Boys School reeks of dread and despair. Charles Manson, a small, frail boy among the larger, tougher students, becomes an easy target. One chilling night, shadowed figures corner him; the air thickens with menace as a staff member lurks nearby, his silent presence giving tacit approval.

The boys grab Manson, throwing him against the cold, hard floor. His cries are muffled by the laughter and jeers of his attackers, the sound echoing off the bare walls.

                    STUDENT #1
               (laughing cruelly)
          Let's see how tough you really are,
          runt.

Manson struggles, but the boys overpower him, their actions fueled by a twisted sense of dominance and the implicit encouragement of the overseeing staff.

INT. SCHOOL YARD - DAY

Day after day, Manson endures repeated beatings. His body bears the bruises and scars of each assault. Determined to protect himself, he devises a bizarre tactic.

As a group approaches, Manson starts his "insane game." He screeches at the top of his lungs, his face contorting into grotesque expressions, arms flailing wildly.

                    CHARLES
               (screaming maniacally)
          Back off! I'll rip your souls out!

The other boys stop, taken aback. Some laugh nervously, unsure how to respond to this madness, giving Manson just enough space to slip away.

EXT. SCHOOL GROUNDS - VARIOUS TIMES

Manson's escapes become frequent, each attempt a desperate bid for freedom. He's caught and returned, only to face harsher punishments each time. Despite the relentless cycle of escape and capture, his spirit remains unbroken, each attempt more daring than the last.

His reputation grows; whispers of his unhinged behavior circulate among both students and staff, creating a buffer of fear and uncertainty that Manson learns to navigate.

INT. INDIANA BOYS SCHOOL - HEADMASTER'S OFFICE - DAY

After his eighteenth failed escape, Manson is dragged before the headmaster, his face a mask of defiance despite his battered condition.

>   HEADMASTER
>   (furiously)
>   What will it take to break you,
>   Manson?
>
>   CHARLES
>   (defiantly)
>   You can't break what's already
>   broken.

The headmaster's face hardens, signaling more punishment to come, but Manson's eyes blaze with a fierce determination to survive, no matter the cost.

EXT. INDIANA BOYS SCHOOL - NIGHT

INSERT CARD: FEBRUARY 1951

In the bleak midwinter, Charles Manson, now 17, and two other students, all cloaked in darkness, make a daring escape from the Indiana Boys School. Their breaths create misty plumes in the freezing air as they hurriedly climb over the perimeter fence, disappearing into the night.

EXT. RURAL ROAD - NIGHT

The trio, fueled by adrenaline and the thrill of freedom, steal their first car from a dimly lit filling station. Manson, taking the driver's seat, steers them towards the promise of California.

INT. STOLEN CAR - DAY

As they drive, the landscape changes from the snowy fields of Indiana to the arid expanses of the Midwest. The boys switch cars frequently, boosting new rides from small-town filling stations. With each stop, they grab snacks and small amounts of cash, each theft making them bolder.

                    CHARLES
              (whispering excitedly)
         Keep your eyes peeled for the next
         one. We need more gas, and a
         better car.

EXT. FILLING STATION - DAY

In a coordinated, now practiced maneuver, the boys pull into
a remote Utah filling station. While one keeps watch, Manson
and the other BOY, 17, rush in. They threaten the lone
attendant, hastily grabbing money from the register and a few
provisions.

                    BOY
              (hastily)
         Let's go, let's go damn it! Cops
         can't be far behind!

EXT. HIGHWAY - DAY

Their stolen car barrels down the highway, the vast, rugged
scenery of Utah unfolding around them. Their freedom is
palpable, but so is the looming threat of capture.

EXT. HIGHWAY - LATER

Sirens blare as state troopers finally catch up. The boys'
car is forced off the road after a tense chase. Surrounded
by police, their brief taste of freedom evaporates as they're
handcuffed beside the car.

                    POLICE OFFICER
              (sternly)
         Thought you could outrun us, huh?

Manson, defiant yet resigned, glances at the barren
landscape, his dream of reaching California dashed as he's
led back to the constraints of the law.

INT. POLICE STATION - DAY

In the stark, fluorescent-lit room of a Utah police station,
Manson and his companions face the consequences of their
cross-state crime spree. The reality of their situation sets
in, marking yet another chapter in Manson's tumultuous life
of fleeting escapes and inevitable captures.

INT. TRANSFER VEHICLE - DAY

Charles Manson is handcuffed, seated next to an AGENT in a
government vehicle speeding along the highway. The agent
glances at Manson, then back to the road.

                    AGENT
               (talking as he drives)
          You know, Manson, crossing state
          lines in a stolen car? That's a
          federal offense. Now you're
          heading to the National Training
          School for Boys in D.C. They deal
          with tough cases like yours.

Manson, gazing out the window, smirks slightly but says
nothing.

                    AGENT (CONT'D)
               (continuing)
          It's not just any reform school,
          kid. They'll test you, try to
          figure out what makes you tick.
          Think you can handle that?

                    CHARLES
               (sarcastically)
          I've handled worse.

The vehicle continues on, the Washington skyline beginning to
appear in the distance.

INT. NATIONAL TRAINING SCHOOL FOR BOYS - INTAKE ROOM - DAY

Manson arrives at the imposing facility, his latest criminal
act marking a significant escalation in his troubled youth.
Upon arrival, he undergoes a series of tests administered by
stern-faced staff who are keen on assessing his potential for
rehabilitation.

INT. TESTING ROOM - DAY

Charles Manson sits at a small desk, pencil in hand, staring
bewilderedly at the test booklet before him. An EXAMINER
observes from across the room.

                    EXAMINER
               (encouragingly)
          Take your time, Charles. Just do
          your best.

Manson scribbles something, then pauses, looking frustrated.

>   CHARLES
>   (muttering)
>   What's the point? These words...
>   they might as well be in another
>   language.

The examiner approaches, noting Manson's struggle.

>   EXAMINER
>   (softly, as he peers over
>   Manson's shoulder)
>   You're having trouble with the
>   reading?

>   CHARLES
>   (defiantly)
>   I ain't stupid, I just... never
>   got the hang of it, alright?

The examiner nods, making a note on his clipboard.

>   EXAMINER
>   (intently)
>   It's alright, Charles. This test
>   shows more than just book smarts.
>   You have a sharp mind—it's clear
>   from how you handle problem-
>   solving. But we need to work on
>   your literacy.

Manson looks up, a mix of surprise and curiosity in his eyes.

>   CHARLES
>   (skeptically)
>   You think you can teach me?

>   EXAMINER
>   (confidently)
>   We can try. Education isn't just
>   about what you've missed; it's
>   about what you can still learn.

Manson considers this, a slight, thoughtful nod showing his
tentative acceptance to try.

INT. CASE WORKER'S OFFICE - DAY

In a sparse, clinical office, Manson sits across from his
CASE WORKER, a middle-aged man with a clipboard, who reviews
the test results with a furrowed brow.

                         CASE WORKER
                    (assessing, not unkindly)
              Charles, your tests show you're
              quite intelligent, but you've got a
              history that's hard to overlook.
              You're illiterate—did you know
              that?

                         CHARLES
                    (defensively)
              Doesn't mean I'm stupid. I know
              things, just not from books.

The case worker notes this, his expression a mix of concern
and professional detachment.

                         CASE WORKER
                    (making notes)
              Your IQ is above average, Charles,
              but your behavior... it's
              aggressively antisocial. We need
              to address that if you're to make
              any progress here.

Manson bristles at the label, his eyes flashing a mix of
defiance and wounded pride.

                         CHARLES
                    (sarcastically)
              Antisocial, huh? Maybe I just
              don't like being pushed around.

The case worker sighs, sensing the deep-seated issues that
lie beneath Manson's tough exterior.

                         CASE WORKER
                    (seriously)
              We're here to help, but you've got
              to be willing to help yourself,
              too.

As Manson is led away to his new quarters, the reality of his
situation sinks in. He is caught in a cycle of incarceration
and fleeting freedom, with each stop providing stark insights
into his complex psyche and the challenges that lie ahead in
managing his behavior.

FLASHBACK:

INT. CALIFORNIA CORCORAN STATE PRISON - 1994

The grainy footage on an old tape rolls, its time code
flickering obscurely at the bottom of the screen. The audio
is muffled, reverberating within the concrete walls.

Charles Manson, aged and weathered, is seated in a simple
wooden chair. He is shackled and handcuffed, his demeanor
oscillating between intense pain and eerie calmness.
Suddenly, from deep within, he emits a prolonged, haunting
wail.

                    CHARLES
               (painfully)
          AWWWW, AWWWW...

His expression shifts abruptly as he sits up straight, his
voice steadying as he speaks to someone off camera.

                    CHARLES (CONT'D)
               (calmly, with a
               philosophical tone)
          Now that's where Rock & Roll comes
          from. And you go on the tier, and
          you sing on the tier, someone hears
          that. They come in there goin'
          ahhhh, ahhhh, and they stay in
          prison 10 or 15 years and when
          they're leaving, they're goin'
          uhhhh, uhhhh...

His tone becomes more animated, his words flowing faster as
he delves deeper into his thoughts.

                    CHARLES (CONT'D)
               (excitedly)
          And, you see it. And know what you
          got, your majesty upside down and
          music comes from the crown. Music
          comes from your King, music comes
          from your Lord, music comes from
          your soul.

His mood darkens, anger seeping into his words as he
critiques the music industry.

                    CHARLES (CONT'D)
               (angrily)
          Hollywood plays music to little
          girls. I don't play little girl
          music. I play music for God; I
          play music for myself. Then when I
          come up with a song and they change
          the words...

Manson's anger peaks as he scowls, his face contorting with
fury. He clenches his jaw, grits his teeth, and stomps his
feet in frustration.

                    CHARLES (CONT'D)
               (furiously)
          I say don't change the words, if
          you change the words my shadows are
          running fast man. I'm running out
          of monks' hood. I'm running out of
          Boys Towns Father Flanagan
          Nebraska. I'm running out of Irish
          Catholic Church man. I'm running
          out of—see what I'm sayin', in
          other words I'm running, I'm
          running from IRA, I'm running out
          of everyone that wants to live on
          the planet Earth man. I'm running
          from nowhere and doing nothing, I'm
          all the same. I'm just such as it
          goes on and on and Shakespeare was
          a clown.

As his rant winds down, Manson's energy seems to drain from
him, leaving him looking more isolated and disconnected than
ever. The camera lingers on his face, a portrait of a man
profoundly at odds with the world.

END FLASHBACK.

INT. PSYCHIATRIST'S OFFICE - DAY

INSERT CARD: OCTOBER 1951

In a clinical yet somewhat comforting office, a psychiatrist
reviews Charles Manson's file. The room is quiet except for
the soft rustling of papers. The PSYCHIATRIST looks
thoughtfully at Manson, who sits across from him, appearing
somewhat anxious.

                    PSYCHIATRIST
               (firmly)
          Charles, based on our sessions and
          your progress, I believe a change
          of environment could be beneficial.
          I'm recommending a transfer to
          Natural Bridge Honor Camp in
          Virginia. It's a minimum-security
          facility, more freedom, more
          opportunities to develop
          positively.

Manson nods, the concept of 'more freedom' resonating with him, a spark of hope visible in his eyes.

EXT. NATURAL BRIDGE HONOR CAMP - DAY

The facility is surrounded by lush forests and rolling hills, a stark contrast to the harsh confines of the previous institutions.

INT. ADMINISTRATION OFFICE - NATURAL BRIDGE HONOR CAMP - DAY

Manson, 17, now in a less restrictive environment, meets with the camp administrators. His demeanor shows cautious optimism. During the meeting, his Aunt Glenna arrives, her expression one of determined support.

                    GLENNA
               (earnestly to the
               administrators)
          I've seen a change in Charles. I
          want to help him once he's ready to
          leave here. He can stay with me,
          and I'll help him find work.

The administrators look at each other, impressed by her commitment. They nod in agreement, seeing this as a positive step toward Manson's rehabilitation.

                    ADMINISTRATOR
               (appreciatively)
          That's very generous of you, ma'am.
          Having a supportive family
          environment can make a significant
          difference.

Manson looks at his aunt, his face softening. For the first time in a long while, he allows himself to feel a small wave of relief and gratitude.

                    GLENNA
               (smiling at Charles)
          We'll get through this together,
          Charles.

The meeting ends with a sense of cautious optimism, the administrators making notes of the plans for Manson's eventual transition to a more stable and supportive environment.

EXT. NATURAL BRIDGE HONOR CAMP - SUNSET

Manson stands at the edge of the camp, looking out over the
natural vistas that surround him. The setting sun casts a
warm glow, and for a moment, he feels the weight of his past
troubles lessen, contemplating a future that might hold
something better.

INT. NATURAL BRIDGE HONOR CAMP - DORMITORY - NIGHT

The dim light casts long shadows across the cold walls.
Charles Manson stands over a young boy, his hand gripping a
knife. The boy's eyes are wide with fear, his body
trembling.

Manson his voice is low and menacing, his breath hot against
the boy's ear.

                    CHARLES
          You're gonna be a good boy for me,
          ain't ya? Gonna do what I say.

The boy nods frantically, tears streaming down his face.
Manson's free hand reaches out, grabbing the boy's chin
roughly.

                    CHARLES (CONT'D)
          That's right. Now, let's have some
          fun-bitch!

He presses the knife against the boy's throat, not hard
enough to break the skin, but enough to make the boy gasp.
The boy's screams echo through the dormitory as Manson tries
to rape him.

The dormitory door suddenly swings open, and a group of
guards rush in. Manson quickly steps back, hiding the knife
behind his back but is quickly subdued and wrestled to the
floor.

INT. NATURAL BRIDGE HONOR CAMP - ADMINISTRATIVE OFFICE - DAY

INSERT CARD: JANUARY 1952

Charles Manson sits nervously across from the camp
superintendent, MR. JOHNSON, 50, a stern man with a stack of
reports on his desk.

                    MR. JOHNSON
               (gravely)
          Charles, we've encountered a
          serious issue.
                    (MORE)

                    MR. JOHNSON (CONT'D)
          There's been an incident involving
          you and another inmate. This type
          of behavior jeopardizes your safety
          and others'.

Manson fidgets, his expression defiant yet anxious.

                    CHARLES
               (defensively)

It wasn't how they're saying. I was just—

                    MR. JOHNSON
               (interrupting)
          I've seen the reports, Charles.
          This goes beyond a simple
          altercation. Given the severity,
          we have no choice but to transfer
          you.

EXT. NATURAL BRIDGE HONOR CAMP - DAY

Manson, handcuffed, is led to a transport vehicle by two
guards. His face is stoic, betraying no emotion as he
glances back at the camp one last time.

INT. FEDERAL REFORMATORY, PETERSBURG, VIRGINIA - INTAKE AREA -
DAY

INSERT CARD: FEDERAL REFORMATORY

Upon arrival at the Federal Reformatory, Manson is processed
by OFFICER DAVIS, male white, 35, who reads through his file
with a look of concern.

                    OFFICER DAVIS
               (skeptically)
          Looks like you're making quite the
          name for yourself.

Manson remains silent, his jaw clenched.

                    OFFICER DAVIS (CONT'D)
          You're on thin ice here. Don't
          expect any leniency.

Manson nods, understanding the gravity of his situation as
he's led away to his new cell.

INT. FEDERAL REFORMATORY - SHOWERS - NIGHT

The steam-filled room echoes with the sounds of dripping
water and distant shouting. Charles Manson stands under a
showerhead, his slender body glistening with water. His eyes
scan the room, settling on a young INMATE washing nearby.

                    CHARLES
              (predatory tone)
          Hey, pretty boy.

Manson approaches the inmate, his movements slow and
deliberate.

                    CHARLES (CONT'D)
          You look like you could use some
          company.

The inmate turns, his eyes widening as he sees Manson. He
stammers, trying to back away.

                    INMATE
          I-I don't want any trouble, Manson.
          Just leave me alone.

Manson chuckles darkly, closing the distance between them.
He presses the inmate against the cold tile wall, his hand
gripping the boy's throat.

                    CHARLES
          Trouble? Nah, I'm just being
          friendly.

INT. FEDERAL REFORMATORY - WARDEN'S OFFICE - DAY

The room is stark and sterile, with a large wooden desk
dominating the space. WARDEN JOHNSON, male white, 50s, sits
behind the desk, his face stern and unforgiving.

Charles Manson sits across from him, his hands cuffed, a
defiant smirk on his face.

                    WARDEN JOHNSON
          Manson, I've called you here to
          discuss your recent...
          indiscretions.

Warden Johnson shuffles a stack of papers, his eyes
narrowing.

                    WARDEN JOHNSON (CONT'D)
          Eight serious disciplinary
          offenses, three of which involve
          homosexual acts. I can't tolerate
          this behavior in my prison.

Manson leaning back in his chair, unfazed.

                    CHARLES
          Oh, come on, Warden. It's not like
          I killed anyone. Just having a
          little fun, you know?

Warden Johnson his face red with anger.

                    WARDEN JOHNSON
          You think rape is fun, Manson? You
          think forcing yourself on other
          inmates is a joke?
                    (He leans forward, his
                     eyes boring into
                     Manson's)
          I've had enough of your antics.
          You're being transferred to the
          maximum-security reformatory at
          Chillicothe, Ohio. And you'll stay
          there until your release on your
          21st birthday.

Manson smirks, unfazed by the warden's outburst.

                    CHARLES
          Chillicothe, huh? Sounds like a
          real party. Maybe I'll make some
          new friends there.

Manson He stands up, the cuffs rattling.

                    CHARLES (CONT'D)
          But hey, at least I'll have plenty
          of time to think about my...
          indiscretions.

Warden Johnson stands up as well, his voice low and menacing.

                    WARDEN JOHNSON
          You think this is a joke, Manson?
          You're a danger to yourself and
          others.

INT. MAXIMUM-SECURITY REFORMATORY, CHILLICOTHE, OHIO - DAY

INSET CARD: CHILLICOTHE REFORMATORY 1952

The gates of the Chillicothe reformatory close heavily behind
CHARLES MANSON, now transferred to this maximum-security
facility due to his repeated offenses and behavior deemed too
risky for less secure environments. The reformatory, known
for its strict regime and imposing architecture, looms large
as Manson is led inside by a GUARD.

> GUARD
> (sternly)
> Welcome to Chillicothe. You'll be
> here till you're 21. Make it easy
> on yourself, follow the rules.

Manson, taking in the high walls and barbed wire, nods
silently, his face set in a grim mask of resignation.

INT. CHILLICOTHE REFORMATORY - CELL BLOCK - DAY

Manson is shown to his cell, a small, stark room with nothing
but a bed, a toilet, and a small window high up on the wall.
He sits on the bed, absorbing the reality of his confinement.

> CHARLES
> (muttering to himself)
> Just gotta make it to '55...

The sound of locks clicking and distant voices echo through
the block, a constant reminder of the strict control under
which he now lives.

INT. CHILLICOTHE REFORMATORY - MESS HALL - DAY

Manson eats his meals surrounded by other inmates, all under
the watchful eyes of guards. Despite the oppressive
environment, he observes everything, learning the unspoken
rules of the inmate hierarchy.

INT. CHILLICOTHE REFORMATORY - YARD - DAY

During yard time, Manson walks alone, keeping to himself.
The cold Ohio wind whips through the yard, but the physical
chill is nothing compared to the isolation he feels. Yet,
this solitude gives him time to think, to plan, to dream of
the day he walks out a free man.

                    CHARLES
               (to himself, resolute)
          I'm not gonna let this place break
          me. I'm getting out, and I'm never
          coming back.

As he looks out beyond the fences, his expression is one of
steely determination, hinting at the complex layers of
thought behind those eyes. The camera pulls back. Manson's
appearance is that of a small figure against the sprawling
confines of the reformatory, counting down the days until his
release.

INT. CHILLICOTHE REFORMATORY - WARDEN'S OFFICE - DAY

INSERT CARD: MAY 1954

Inside the somber office, CHARLES MANSON sits across from the
WARDEN, a stoic white man in his 50s with a reputation for
fairness. The warden reviews Manson's file, noting the
marked improvement in his behavior.

                    WARDEN
               (looking up from the file)
          Charles, it seems you've made some
          real progress. Your conduct report
          shows significant improvement. How
          do you feel about going home?

Manson, a bit taken aback by the sudden prospect of freedom,
nods cautiously.

                    CHARLES
               (hesitantly)
          I'm ready, sir. I've thought a lot
          about this day.

                    WARDEN
               (nodding)
          Good. We've arranged for you to be
          released into the custody of your
          aunt and uncle in West Virginia.
          They're willing to support you and
          help you adjust back into society.

Manson's face softens, a mix of relief and uncertainty
crossing his features.

                    CHARLES
               (gratefully)
          Thank you, sir. I won't let them
          down.

EXT. CHILLICOTHE REFORMATORY - GATES - DAY

The gates of the reformatory open, and Manson steps out into
the bright daylight of early May, his few belongings in a
small bag. He looks back at the imposing structure one last
time before turning his face towards the future.

EXT. WEST VIRGINIA - THOMAS RESIDENCE - DAY

Manson arrives at the modest home of his Aunt Glenna and
Uncle Bill. Glenna greets him at the door with a cautious
smile, extending a hand to welcome him.

                    GLENNA
               (softly)
          Welcome home, Charles. We're here
          to help you get back on your feet.

Uncle Bill stands a few steps behind, nodding sternly but
with a welcoming warmth in his eyes.

                    BILL
               (just audible)
          Make yourself at home, boy. Fresh
          start.

As Manson steps into the house, he feels a mix of nostalgia
and new beginnings. The familiar smells and sights of his
aunt and uncle's home bring back memories of a simpler time
before his incarcerations.

INT. THOMAS RESIDENCE - CHARLES' NEW ROOM - DAY

Manson unpacks his belongings in a small, tidy room. He
arranges his few possessions with care, each movement
deliberate. Sitting on the edge of the bed, he takes a deep
breath, ready to embrace this new chapter.

                    CHARLES
               (to himself, determined)
          This is it. Time to start over.
          For real this time.

Manson looks out of the window, his gaze set on the peaceful
West Virginia landscape, a symbol of his hopes for redemption
and a normal life.

INT. SMALL WEDDING CHAPEL - DAY

INSERT CARD: JANUARY 1955

In a modest chapel, CHARLES MANSON, 21, stands beside ROSALIE
"ROSIE" JEAN WILLIS, a white 16-year-old hospital waitress.

The setting is humble, with a few close friends and family in
attendance. The couple exchanges vows, a hopeful smile on
Rosalie's face reflecting her love and optimism.

                    ROSALIE
               (softly, to Charles)
          I believe in us, Charles.

Manson, visibly moved, nods. He seems committed, wanting to
forge a new path.

EXT. LOS ANGELES - DAY

INSERT CARD: OCTOBER 1955

The newlyweds arrive in Los Angeles in a car that Manson had
stolen in Ohio. The city's sprawling expanse feels like a
fresh start but carries undertones of the challenges they
face.

INT. MANSON'S APARTMENT - LOS ANGELES - DAY

Rosalie, now visibly pregnant, watches as Manson paces
nervously. He's anxious about their future, especially after
learning that federal agents are investigating the stolen
car.

                    CHARLES
               (worried)
          They're on to me about the car. I
          thought we were safe here.

Rosalie tries to console him, but the stress is palpable.

INT. COURTROOM - LOS ANGELES - DAY

Manson, concern washes over him. He stands before a JUDGE,
male white 50s, after looking at court documents, the Judge
pulls down his glasses and addresses Manson.

                    JUDGE
               (sternly)
          You were given a psychiatric
          evaluation. I'm handing down five
          years' probation for transporting a
          stolen vehicle across state lines.
                    (MORE)

                    JUDGE (CONT'D)
          This is your chance, Mr. Manson.
          Any further missteps, and you'll
          face severe consequences.

EXT. LOS ANGELES STREET - DAY

INSERT CARD: MARCH 1956

While walking with his wife Rosalie, a police squad car spots
Manson. The cops pull over and stop Manson, they place him
in handcuffs.

                    CHARLES
          Ay, man, what are you doing?

                    COP
          You're under arrest.

                    CHARLES
          For what?

                    COP
          You have a warrant. Failure to
          appear in court.

                    CHARLES
          Aw, that's bullshit man.

Manson is arrested once again. He's led away by police, his
despair evident as Rosalie watches, distraught.

INT. COURTROOM - DAY

Back in court, Manson stands before the judge, visibly angry,
as he receives a scolding.

                    JUDGE
               (firmly)
          You have wasted your opportunities,
          Mr. Manson. Your failure to appear
          at a hearing for a similar charge
          filed in Florida led to your arrest
          in Indianapolis in March 1956.
          Therefore, I am revoking your
          probation and sentencing you to
          three years at Terminal Island
          prison in Los Angeles.

Manson is taken away, his fleeting moments of freedom ending
as he faces the reality of his actions.

EXT. TERMINAL ISLAND - DAY

The foreboding structure of Terminal Island looms as Manson
is escorted inside. The gates close behind him, signaling
the start of another challenging chapter in his tumultuous
life.

INT. TERMINAL ISLAND PRISON - DAY

In the somber confines of Terminal Island, Charles Manson
sits alone in his cell when a GUARD approaches, a slip of
paper in hand.

                    GUARD
              (solemnly)
          Manson, you have a son. Charles
          Manson Jr. Born today.

Manson, caught between joy and sorrow, nods silently, the
weight of fatherhood settling amidst his incarceration.

INT. TERMINAL ISLAND - VISITATION ROOM - VARIOUS DAYS

Throughout his first year, the visitation room becomes a
place of mixed emotions for Manson. Rosalie, weary yet
resilient, visits with their newborn son, offering Manson a
glimpse of the life he's missing.

Rosalie struggles to maintain a brave face, her resolve
hardening with each visit.

                    ROSALIE
              (trying to stay positive)
          He's growing fast, Charles. Looks
          like you.

Manson reaches out, fingers brushing the glass that separates
them, a physical reminder of the barriers between him and his
new family.

Ada, now 37, joins Rosalie on some visits, providing support.
She sits beside her daughter-in-law, her face lined with the
hardships of the years but eyes hopeful.

                    ADA
              (encouragingly)
          We're here for you, Charlie. We're
          taking care of little Charlie too.

As the months pass, the visits from Rosalie become less
frequent.

The strain of raising a child alone, the stigma of Manson's crimes, and the bleak reality of her situation begin to erode her resolve.

INT. TERMINAL ISLAND - CHARLES MANSON'S CELL - NIGHT

Manson lies awake at night, the silence of the cell block echoing the turmoil in his mind. The joy of new fatherhood clashes with the pain of his separation and the reality of his circumstances. Each visit reinforces what he stands to lose and the life he might never fully know.

The narrative weaves through these visits, charting Manson's emotional journey within the prison walls, underscored by the stark contrast between his grim reality and the outside world, where life continues relentlessly.

INT. TERMINAL ISLAND PRISON - VISITATION ROOM - DAY

INSERT CARD: MARCH 1957

Charles Manson sits expectantly in the visitation room, a place that once brought him fleeting moments of joy. Today, however, the atmosphere is heavy, tense. The room feels colder, emptier without Rosalie and his son. His mother, Ada, arrives alone, her expression solemn, carrying news Manson dreads but anticipates.

                    ADA
          (softly, hesitantly)
     Charlie, Rosalie isn't coming
     anymore... She's... she's with
     someone else now, living with
     another man.

Manson's face hardens, the news striking him like a physical blow. He looks away, clenching his fists in an attempt to control the surge of emotion.

                    CHARLES
          (bitterly)
     Shit, I knew it... I knew this
     would happen.

Ada reaches out, touching the glass that separates them, her voice cracking with maternal concern.

                    ADA
          (gently)
     I'm so sorry, Charlie. We're still
     here for you, your son and I.

Manson barely nods, his thoughts swirling with betrayal and frustration.

INT. TERMINAL ISLAND PRISON - CELL BLOCK - NIGHT

In the days following, Manson's demeanor darkens. The news festers, and his mind races for a way out. Less than two weeks before his scheduled parole hearing, driven by despair and desperation, he makes a rash decision.

INT. TERMINAL ISLAND PRISON - GARAGE - NIGHT

Manson sneaks into the prison garage, a poorly lit, grim area filled with prison maintenance vehicles. He hot-wires one of the cars, the engine sputtering to life under his hurried hands. His heart pounds as he drives toward the exit, a fleeting hope of freedom igniting within him.

EXT. TERMINAL ISLAND PRISON - GATES - NIGHT

The escape is short-lived. Alarms blare, lights flash, and guards swiftly intercept him just as he nears the gate. Manson is pulled from the car, his brief taste of freedom evaporating as quickly as it appeared.

INT. PRISON ADMINISTRATIVE OFFICE - DAY

Back in the administrative office, Manson faces the consequences of his actions. The parole board is unimpressed by his escape attempt, especially so close to his parole hearing.

                    PAROLE BOARD OFFICIAL
               (sternly)
          Given your recent actions, your
          parole is denied. Furthermore, you
          are sentenced to an additional five
          years' probation for this escape
          attempt.

Manson sits, defeated, as the reality of his continued imprisonment sinks in. The walls of the prison feel even more constricting, the weight of his choices heavier than ever.

INT. TERMINAL ISLAND PRISON - ADMINISTRATOR'S OFFICE - DAY

INSERT CARD: SEPTEMBER 1958

Charles Manson, now 24, sits across from the prison
administrator in a sparse, bureaucratic office. The air is
filled with the heavy anticipation of freedom and the
underlying tension of re-entering society.

>   PRISON ADMINISTRATOR
>   (officially)
>   You're being released today,
>   Manson. You'll be on parole for
>   the next five years. Remember, any
>   slip-ups, and you could be back
>   here.

Manson nods, a complex mix of emotions crossing his
face—relief, uncertainty, and a trace of defiance.

>   CHARLES
>   (resolutely)
>   I understand. You won't see me
>   here again.

He signs the release papers, each stroke of the pen etching
the finality of his prison term and the beginning of his
conditional freedom.

EXT. TERMINAL ISLAND PRISON - GATES - DAY

Manson steps out of the prison gates, squinting in the bright
sunlight of freedom. He takes a deep breath of fresh air,
his expression one of someone who's spent too long in
confinement.

INT. LOS ANGELES - DIVORCE COURT - DAY (SAME YEAR)

Elsewhere, Rosalie Willis, now estranged from Manson, sits in
a divorce court. The judge finalizes their divorce, granting
her a decree. Rosalie's face is a mixture of sadness and
relief, closing a tumultuous chapter in her life.

>   ROSALIE
>   (softly, to her lawyer)
>   It's finally over.

The lawyer nods sympathetically, handing her the official
papers.

EXT. LOS ANGELES STREETS - DAY

Manson wanders the streets, a free man yet bound by the
conditions of his parole. He watches families and couples
pass by, their normalcy a stark contrast to the isolation and
turmoil he feels within. The reality of his solitude and the
challenges of reintegrating into society weigh heavily on him
as he contemplates his next steps.

                    CHARLES
               (to himself)
          What now?

As he walks into the uncertain future, Manson is at a
crossroads, determined to find a new path but haunted by the
shadows of his past.

EXT. LOS ANGELES STREET - NIGHT

The neon lights of the city cast a garish glow on the faces
of the people walking the streets. Charles Manson leans
against a lamppost, his eyes scanning the crowd. A young
GIRL, no older than 16, approaches him, her makeup heavy and
her clothes revealing.

                    GIRL
          Hey, Charlie. I got a john for
          you. He's waiting in his car.

She nods towards a sleek, expensive-looking vehicle parked
nearby.

                    CHARLES
               (smirks, lighting a
                cigarette)
          Good girl. You're learning.

Manson takes a drag, his eyes narrowing.

                    CHARLES (CONT'D)
          And the other girl? The rich one?
          Has she come through with the cash?

                    GIRL
          Yeah, she wired you the money like
          you asked. Said her parents are
          out of town, so we can use her
          place tonight.

Manson takes another drag of his cigarette, a satisfied grin
spreading across his face.

                    CHARLES
          Perfect. Looks like we're in
          business, sweetheart. Tonight's
          gonna be a good night.

There is an unsettling image of Manson and the young girl,
their plans for the evening shrouded in darkness and
implications.

INT. COURTROOM - DAY (SEPTEMBER 1959)

In a solemn courtroom, CHARLES MANSON stands before the
judge, his expression a mix of anxiety and resignation.

                    JUDGE
          Mr. Manson. You have been charged
          with attempting to cash a forged
          U.S. Treasury check and theft.
          Stealing the check from a mailbox

His attorney presents the defense, quickly intervenes.

                    DEFENSE ATTORNEY
              (earnestly)
          Your Honor, Mr. Manson has
          acknowledged his mistake. He is
          ready to rectify his actions and
          contribute positively to society.

Manson nods slightly, his gaze turning to LEONA RAE "CANDY"
STEVENS, female white, 21, who steps forward, her demeanor
nervous yet determined.

                    LEONA RAE CANDY STEVENS
              (tearfully)
          Your Honor, I know Charles has made
          mistakes, but we are deeply in
          love. We plan to marry, and I
          believe together we can create a
          new path for him.

The judge listens intently, moved by her emotional plea. The
courtroom is tense, the air thick with the gravity of her
words.

                         JUDGE
                    (considering)
               Given the circumstances and the
               dismissal of the theft charge, I am
               inclined to offer Mr. Manson a
               chance for rehabilitation outside
               of prison. I'm handing down a ten-
               year suspended sentence and
               probation.

Manson, who sighs deeply, a look of relief washing over him
as he glances at Candy.

EXT. COURTHOUSE - DAY

Outside the courthouse, Manson and Candy embrace, surrounded
by the buzz of the city. Candy's face shows a mixture of
relief and worry, aware of the weight of her testimony and
its consequences.

                         CHARLES
                    (gratefully)
               Thank you, Candy. You didn't have
               to do that.

                         CANDY
                    (softly)
               I did. We're in this together now,
               Charlie.

INT. SMALL CHAPEL - DAY

In a quiet, dimly lit chapel, Charles Manson and Leona Rae
"Candy" Stevens stand before a hurriedly arranged officiant.
Sparse decorations and a lack of guests underscore the
urgency and secrecy of the ceremony. The couple exchanges
vows in a muted, tense atmosphere, each aware of the legal
and emotional complexities sealing their union.

FLASHBACK:

INT. CALIFORNIA CORCORAN STATE PRISON - 1994

A grainy, flickering video plays, resembling an old VHS
recording. The time code at the bottom of the screen is
faded and nearly illegible. The audio is distorted, heavy
with reverb, making the words echo eerily within the stark
prison room.

Charles Manson sits in a rigid wooden chair, shackled at the
wrists and waist.

His long, unkempt hair and grizzled beard give him an almost biblical appearance. His eyes, intense and unwavering, stare straight ahead, his expression unreadable yet charged with unspoken energy.

Behind him, TWO PRISON GUARDS stand stiffly against the wall, watching cautiously, their postures rigid with unease.

Manson's hands twitch within the cuffs as he shifts slightly, the chains clinking softly. He breathes deeply before speaking, his voice deliberate, heavy with conviction.

                    MANSON
          Uh, I don't know, this is very
          intricate, man.

He pauses, his gaze flickering slightly before he continues, his tone shifting to one of conspiratorial certainty.

                    MANSON (CONT'D)
          The black hand... it comes from
          the Catholic Church. The Romans
          have been using it for years. The
          black hand is, supposedly, the hand
          of God from the cross... but it's
          really upside down.

His body subtly tenses, his eyes narrowing as his words take on a deeper intensity.

                    MANSON (CONT'D)
          It comes from the negros... the
          slaves that Abraham Lincoln played
          with.

Manson's words linger in the air, twisted logic woven into historical references, his voice an eerie mixture of authority and delusion. The video crackles slightly, the reverb making his words swirl hauntingly in the confined space. The unseen interviewer remains silent, offering no challenge, no acknowledgment—just the void absorbing his monologue.

END FLASHBACK.

INT. MOTEL ROOM - ALBUQUERQUE, NEW MEXICO - NIGHT

A dingy motel room, dimly lit by a flickering neon sign outside the window. Charles Manson sits on the edge of the bed, smoking a cigarette, his restless energy filling the cramped space. Across from him, Leona Rae "Candy" Stevens and another YOUNG WOMAN lounge on the bed, their body language tense yet compliant.

Manson exhales a slow stream of smoke, his mind always working, always scheming.

                    CHARLES
              (low, persuasive)
         This is how we get by, baby. It
         ain't about the money, it's about
         control. About knowing how to play
         the game.

Candy glances at the other woman, uncertainty flickering across her face. She knows better than to argue with him, but something about this situation feels off.

                    LEONA RAE CANDY STEVENS
              (skeptical)
         Charlie, are you sure this is safe?
         We barely made it out of California
         without trouble.

Manson waves her concern away, his expression amused but firm.

                    CHARLES
              (smirking)
         Relax, doll. New Mexico's wide
         open. Nobody's paying attention.
         We keep moving, we keep playing it
         smart, we'll be fine.

The young woman shifts uncomfortably. Manson notices, his sharp eyes locking onto her.

                    CHARLES (CONT'D)
              (leaning in, voice softer)
         You scared? Ain't nothing to be
         scared of. Just stick to the plan.

EXT. HIGHWAY OUTSIDE ALBUQUERQUE - NIGHT

A dusty stretch of road. A BLACK SEDAN idles near a truck stop. The neon glow of a roadside diner flickers in the distance. Manson watches from the car as Leona approaches a waiting MAN in a suit. The deal is quick, routine. She disappears into the truck stop with him.

Manson leans back, satisfied, until he spots a pair of headlights in the rearview mirror. A car slowly rolls up behind them. A moment later, RED AND BLUE LIGHTS flash, slicing through the darkness.

                    CHARLES
                (under his breath)
          Damn it...

EXT. MOTEL PARKING LOT - LATER

Manson, Leona, and the young woman are pressed against the
hood of a patrol car, their hands cuffed behind their backs.
A FEDERAL AGENT flips through a notebook, shaking his head.

                    FEDERAL AGENT
                (flatly)
          Mann Act violation. Transporting
          women across state lines for
          prostitution.

Manson smirks despite the situation, the silver bracelets
tight around his wrists.

                    CHARLES
                (chuckling)
          Man, you guys got it all wrong...

The agents aren't amused. The back door of the patrol car
swings open. Manson glances at Leona, her face pale with
fear, before he's shoved inside, the door slamming shut
behind him.

INT. MOTEL ROOM - LOS ANGELES - NIGHT (1960)

A dimly lit motel room. Charles Manson, 26, paces near the
window, peering through the blinds. The room is
cluttered—cigarette butts in an ashtray, a half-eaten
sandwich on the nightstand. Leona Rae "Candy" Stevens sits
on the edge of the bed, fidgeting nervously.

                    LEONA RAE CANDY STEVENS
                (whispering)
          Charlie, you're free. Why not lay
          low, stay clean?

Manson scoffs, shaking his head.

                    CHARLES
                (smirking)
          You really think they're done with
          me? They let me out, but I can
          feel it. They're still watching.

He taps the blinds, eyes darting as if expecting someone
outside.

>   LEONA
>   (pleading)
>   If you run, they'll come after you.
>   Just stay put, do your probation.

Manson turns to her, his expression shifting from amusement to cold determination.

>   CHARLES
>   (scoffing)
>   Stay put? That's a trap, Candy.
>   The Feds don't let guys like me
>   walk. I gotta keep moving.

Leona looks away, knowing there's no stopping him. Manson grabs a small bag, stuffing in a few clothes and a wad of cash. He kisses her on the forehead, then heads for the door.

EXT. BUS STATION - NIGHT

Manson moves through the terminal, keeping his head low. He buys a ticket with cash, disappearing onto a bus heading east. The doors shut, and the vehicle pulls away, his future once again uncertain.

INT. FEDERAL OFFICE - LOS ANGELES - DAY (APRIL 1960)

A group of federal agents gather around a desk cluttered with case files. One agent slaps down a paper—A BENCH WARRANT for Charles Manson.

>   FEDERAL AGENT #1
>   (serious)
>   He's gone. Disappeared right under
>   our noses.

>   FEDERAL AGENT #2
>   (nodding)
>   We knew he'd run. Time to make it
>   official.

The agent picks up a stamp and slams it onto an indictment form—VIOLATION OF THE MANN ACT. The room is quiet for a moment as the weight of the decision settles. The hunt for Manson is back on.

EXT. MOTEL PARKING LOT - HOUSTON, TEXAS - NIGHT (JUNE 1960)

A lone streetlight casts long shadows across the cracked pavement.

A WOMAN, one of Manson's associates, stands near a motel entrance, speaking with a prospective client. The air is thick with humidity, the neon glow of a nearby sign flickering erratically.

SUDDENLY—police vehicles screech to a stop. Officers rush in, guns drawn.

> OFFICER
> (shouting)
> Hands where we can see them!

The woman freezes, realizing it's over. She's thrown against the hood of a squad car, cuffed as another officer rummages through her purse. He pulls out a roll of cash and a motel room key.

> OFFICER #2
> (smirking)
> Looks like we found our missing
> link.

EXT. LAREDO, TEXAS - BORDER PATROL CHECKPOINT - DAY

Charles Manson sits in the driver's seat of an old, dust-covered sedan, inching toward a checkpoint. He wipes sweat from his brow, his fingers tapping anxiously against the steering wheel.

A BORDER PATROL OFFICER leans in through the window.

> BORDER PATROL OFFICER
> (casual)
> Where you headed?

> CHARLES
> (flatly)
> New Orleans.

The officer narrows his eyes, noticing the nervous twitch in Manson's jaw. Another agent approaches the car, motioning to Manson to step out. Within seconds—HE'S SURROUNDED.

> BORDER PATROL OFFICER
> (serious)
> Step out of the vehicle, sir.
> Hands where we can see them.

Manson exhales sharply, knowing he's been caught. He steps out, hands raised, as two officers grab him and slap on cuffs.

INT. LOS ANGELES COURTROOM - DAY

Manson stands before the judge, his smirk barely concealing
his frustration. His attorney is tense beside him, already
knowing the outcome. The JUDGE, an older man with a severe
expression, reads from the case file.

                    JUDGE
               (sternly)
          Mr. Manson, you were given a
          chance. Instead of following the
          terms of your parole, you engaged
          in further criminal activity. For
          violating your probation, I am
          ordering you to serve your original
          ten-year sentence.

Manson's smirk fades. The weight of the judge's words sinks
in.

Bailiffs approach, securing Manson as the judge slams his
gavel. The courtroom murmurs as he is led away, chains
rattling against the floor. He glances back, his expression
unreadable, before being taken through the doors—to prison
once again.

INT. LOS ANGELES COUNTY JAIL - PRISON CELL - NIGHT (JULY 1960
- JULY 1961)

A dim, claustrophobic prison cell. Charles Manson sits on
his cot, staring at a pile of legal documents spread across
his lap. The ink is smudged in places from his restless
fingers thumbing through them over and over. His appeal has
been denied—again.

Manson slams the papers onto the cold concrete floor,
frustration bubbling beneath the surface. His bunkmate, a
disinterested older inmate, watches from the top bunk as
Manson rubs his temples, mumbling to himself.

                    CHARLES
               (muttering)
          Fucking system... stacking the
          deck against me. Ain't no way
          outta this shit.

Manson picks up a pencil and begins scrawling in the margins
of his appeal documents—nonsense phrases, lyrics, symbols.
Anything to keep his mind from unraveling further.

EXT. LOS ANGELES COUNTY JAIL - PRISON TRANSPORT AREA - DAY

INSERT CARD: JULY 1960

A line of shackled prisoners is led onto a fortified prison transport bus. Manson, hands cuffed in front of him, squints against the harsh California sun as a prison guard pushes him forward.

                    PRISON GUARD
               (gruffly)
          Keep moving, Manson. Your new
          home's waiting for you.

The doors shut with a metallic clang, and the bus roars to life, pulling away from the facility. Manson leans against the window, watching as the Los Angeles skyline fades in the distance, his future now bound to the cold isolation of McNeil Island Penitentiary in Washington State.

EXT. MCNEIL ISLAND PENITENTIARY - DAY

A foreboding, fortress-like prison sits on a remote island in Washington's Puget Sound. The air is damp and heavy with mist. A ferry approaches, carrying newly arrived inmates, including Manson. As the boat docks, the guards herd the prisoners onto the island like cattle.

INT. MCNEIL ISLAND PENITENTIARY - INTAKE ROOM - DAY

Manson is processed, his new prison number assigned, his belongings stripped away. The environment is harsher than Terminal Island—less noise, fewer distractions, just the weight of isolation pressing against the cold stone walls.

A prison guard hands him a uniform and a prison-issued Bible, scoffing as he reads through Manson's file.

                    PRISON GUARD
               (chuckling)
          Good luck, preacher boy. Looks
          like you got a lot of repenting to
          do.

Manson smirks but says nothing, his mind already drifting to ways he can manipulate this new world to his advantage.

INT. MCNEIL ISLAND PENITENTIARY - PRISON YARD - DAY

INSERT CARD: LATER THAT YEAR

Manson, now more acclimated to prison life, sits at a
makeshift table in the yard with fellow inmate LANIER RAMER,
29, a hardened man with sharp eyes and an aura of control.
Books and handwritten notes cover the table, pages marked
with symbols and cryptic annotations.

               LANIER
          (leaning in)
     See, Charlie, it's all about
     controlling the mind. That's what
     Scientology teaches—understanding
     the mind, mastering it.

Manson, always drawn to anything that promises influence and
power, listens intently, absorbing every word like scripture.

               CHARLES
          (nodding)
     Yeah... yeah, I see what you're
     saying. Control. That's what it's
     about.

Rayner pushes a worn copy of a Scientology book toward him.
Manson flips through the pages, the words washing over him in
a way no religious text ever had before.

INT. MCNEIL ISLAND PENITENTIARY - PRISON CELL - NIGHT (JULY
1961)

Manson, lying on his cot, scribbles in a notebook. He
pauses, looking up at the ceiling, his mind racing with new
ideas, new philosophies. The prison's monotonous hum
surrounds him, but inside his mind, a new world is taking
shape.

A prison guard walks by, pausing at his cell door.

               PRISON GUARD
          (sarcastic)
     Heard you put down 'Scientology' as
     your religion, Manson. You find
     God or somethin'?

Manson smirks, never breaking eye contact.

               CHARLES
          (chuckling)
     Something like that.

INT. PRISON ADMINISTRATIVE OFFICE - REVIEW BOARD MEETING - DAY

INSERT CARD: SEPTEMBER 1961

A group of PRISON OFFICIALS sits around a table, flipping through a thick file labeled MANSON, CHARLES. The head of the board, an older administrator, adjusts his glasses as he reads aloud.

> BOARD MEMBER #1
> (reading)
> "Appears to have developed a certain amount of insight into his problems through his study of this discipline."

A younger administrator, skeptical, scoffs as he flips through additional reports.

> BOARD MEMBER #2
> (dryly)
> Sounds like he's just found another way to make himself the center of attention.

> BOARD MEMBER #1
> (nodding)
> His file says as much. "Tremendous drive to call attention to himself."

The group exchanges knowing glances. They recognize Manson's behavior for what it is—yet another performance, another act in his endless quest for control.

INT. MCNEIL ISLAND PENITENTIARY - PRISON CHAPEL - DAY

Manson, now fully immersed in his latest fascination, preaches to a small group of inmates in the prison chapel. His words are hypnotic, his delivery compelling. He gestures grandly, speaking in riddles and metaphors, his voice laced with conviction.

> CHARLES
> (sermon-like)
> Man, you gotta understand—this world ain't real. It's a prison inside a prison. But your mind? Your mind can escape. That's what they don't want you to know.

Some inmates nod along, while others merely watch, studying him with curiosity. Manson's intense gaze relishes attention, his words shaping a new persona—one that will define him for decades to come.

INT. MCNEIL ISLAND PENITENTIARY - PRISON YARD - DAY (1962-1966)

A thick layer of mist rolls in from the Puget Sound, coating the concrete prison yard in a damp chill. Charles Manson sits on a worn-out bench, a battered guitar resting on his lap. His fingers stumble over the strings, awkward and clumsy. Across from him, a man watches with mild amusement—ALVIN "CREEPY" KARPIS, 54, an aging yet still imposing figure, a legendary criminal from the Barker-Karpis gang.

Karpis lets out a dry chuckle, shaking his head as Manson fumbles another chord.

> KARPIS
> (grinning)
> Jesus, Charlie. You're butchering that thing.

Manson scowls, adjusting his grip on the guitar.

> CHARLES
> (defensive)
> I ain't had no real teacher, man.
> Ain't like I got a radio in my cell.

Karpis leans forward, taking the guitar from Manson's hands. His calloused fingers move effortlessly over the strings, plucking out a smooth, bluesy progression. Manson watches, eyes locked onto Karpis' hands, absorbing every movement.

> KARPIS
> (smirking)
> It ain't about the fingers. It's about the feel. You gotta let the music move through you.

Manson nods, taking the guitar back. This time, he follows Karpis' example, his playing slightly smoother, more controlled. Karpis grins, sensing potential.

> KARPIS (CONT'D)
> (encouraging)
> That's better, kid. Keep at it, and maybe you'll make something outta yourself after all.

Manson smirks, soaking in the praise. For the first time in years, he's found something that makes him feel important.

INT. MCNEIL ISLAND PENITENTIARY - PRISON LIBRARY - NIGHT

Manson sits at a library table, a tattered notepad in front of him, scribbling lyrics and song ideas between the worn pages of a Scientology book. Around him, other inmates shuffle through the stacks, lost in their own escape from the monotony of prison life.

A figure slides into the seat across from him—an older inmate, a well-connected hustler. He places a small slip of paper on the table and taps it twice.

                    INMATE
              (quietly)
         That's your golden ticket, Charlie.

Manson picks up the slip, scanning the name—PHIL KAUFMAN, UNIVERSAL STUDIOS, HOLLYWOOD. His eyes flick up to the inmate, wary yet intrigued.

                    CHARLES
              (suspicious)
         How'd you get this?

                    INMATE
              (shrugging)
         Don't worry about it. Just know
         Kaufman's a guy who knows people.
         A real mover. You ever make it
         outta here, he's the kinda guy you
         wanna call.

Manson tucks the slip into his pocket, his mind already spinning with possibilities. A connection to Hollywood. A chance at something bigger than prison walls.

EXT. DINER - TACOMA, WASHINGTON - DAY

A greasy spoon diner, its neon sign buzzing in the damp Washington air. Inside, Ada Manson, now in her 40s, moves between tables, refilling coffee cups and taking orders. Her hair is streaked with gray, her face lined with the exhaustion of a life spent surviving.

She pauses at the counter, looking out the window at the rain-slicked streets, her mind drifting to her son, locked away on McNeil Island. She had moved to Washington to be closer to him, taking whatever work she could find, hoping—maybe foolishly—that she could still be part of his life.

A CUSTOMER interrupts her thoughts, waving for the check.
She forces a smile and continues working, the hope in her
eyes dulled but not yet extinguished.

INT. MCNEIL ISLAND PENITENTIARY - PRISON CHAPEL - DAY

Manson sits in the back of the prison chapel, flipping idly
through a book on Scientology. Around him, other inmates
pray or meditate, each seeking their own kind of salvation.

A GUARD approaches, glancing at the book in Manson's hands.

                    GUARD
               (smirking)
          Scientologist now, huh?

Manson looks up, grinning slightly.

                    CHARLES
               (mocking)
          Yeah, man. I found the light.
          Cleared my thetan and everything.

The guard chuckles, shaking his head before walking off.
Manson's grin fades as he turns back to his book, not reading
the words but contemplating what this new label can do for
him. Another tool, another identity to wield.

INT. PRISON ADMINISTRATIVE OFFICE - DAY

INSERT CARD: SEPTEMBER 1962 PSYCHIATRIC REVIEW

A small, sterile office lined with files and manila folders.
A PRISON PSYCHIATRIST flips through Charles Manson's
extensive case file. Across from him, Manson slouches in a
chair, an amused smirk tugging at the corners of his lips.

                    PSYCHIATRIST
               (reading aloud)
          "Deep-seated personality problems."

Manson snickers, shifting in his chair.

                    CHARLES
               (mocking)
          That's a new one. What's that
          supposed to mean?

                    PSYCHIATRIST
               (flatly)
          It means you manipulate.
                    (MORE)

                    PSYCHIATRIST (CONT'D)
          You perform. You pretend to have
          insight, but it's all for show.

Manson's smile widens, but his eyes remain cold.

                    CHARLES
               (chuckling)
          Ain't that what life is? One big
          performance?

The psychiatrist watches him for a long moment, then writes
something down in the file.

                    PSYCHIATRIST
               (serious)
          You have a tremendous drive to call
          attention to yourself, Manson.
          Everything you do—every label you
          adopt, every new philosophy you
          claim to believe—it's all about
          control.

Manson leans forward, clasping his hands together.

                    CHARLES
               (grinning)
          You're catching on, doc.

The psychiatrist exhales, closing the file.

INT. COURTHOUSE - WEST VIRGINIA - DAY (1963)

A sterile courtroom filled with the muted shuffling of papers
and the low murmur of voices. Leona Rae "Candy" Stevens, now
visibly older and weary, sits at a table beside her ATTORNEY.
Across the room, an empty chair looms—Charles Manson is
absent. He remains incarcerated, his presence only felt
through the legal documents stacked neatly in front of the
JUDGE.

Leona fidgets with the hem of her dress, her knuckles white
as she grips the edge of the table. The CLERK calls the
case.

                    CLERK
               (clearing throat)
          Case number 1963-0145. Stevens v.
          Manson. Petition for dissolution
          of marriage.

The judge, an older man with a lined face, adjusts his
glasses as he skims through the divorce papers.

                    JUDGE
               (to Leona's attorney)
          The respondent, Charles Manson, is
          currently incarcerated at McNeil
          Island Penitentiary. He has not
          contested the divorce, correct?

                    LEONA'S ATTORNEY
               (nodding)
          That is correct, Your Honor. My
          client has had no contact with Mr.
          Manson in over a year. She seeks
          full custody of their child and
          wishes to legally sever all ties
          with him.

Murmurs ripple through the courtroom at the mention of a
child. The judge pauses, lifting his eyes from the papers.

                    JUDGE
               (raising an eyebrow)
          A child? There is no record of Mr.
          Manson acknowledging a son.

Leona clears her throat, her voice wavering slightly as she
speaks.

                    LEONA
               (softly)
          Yes, Your Honor. We have a son.
          Charles Luther Manson. He's nearly
          three years old now.

A hushed silence fills the courtroom. The weight of the
revelation lingers as the judge exhales deeply and leans
forward, steepling his fingers.

                    JUDGE
               (skeptically)
          Has Mr. Manson provided any support
          for the child?

                    LEONA
               (shaking her head)
          No, sir. He's never met him.
          Never sent money. Nothing.

                    JUDGE
               (flatly)
          And you believe it is in the
          child's best interest that Mr.
          Manson has no legal or custodial
          rights?

                    LEONA
                (emphatically)
        Yes, Your Honor. I want my son to
        grow up without... without any of
        that in his life.

The judge looks at her for a long moment, then back down at
the paperwork. With a curt nod, he lifts his gavel.

                    JUDGE
        Very well. Divorce is granted.
        Sole custody of the minor child is
        awarded to the petitioner. Mr.
        Manson's parental rights are
        revoked.

The gavel slams down. Final. Absolute. The courtroom
breathes again.

INT. PRISON CELL - MCNEIL ISLAND PENITENTIARY - NIGHT (1963)

A dimly lit prison cell. Charles Manson sits on the edge of
his cot, flipping through a legal notice that had been handed
to him earlier in the day. His lips press into a thin line
as he reads the verdict of the divorce case.

"Petition for dissolution of marriage granted."

"Custody of minor child awarded to petitioner."

"Parental rights revoked."

Manson snorts, tossing the paper onto the floor. He leans
back against the cold cement wall, his mind churning. His
eyes flicker with something unreadable—resentment?
Indifference? The emotions seem fleeting, like passing
shadows. His CELL MATE peers down from the top bunk.

                    CELL MATE
        What's that?

                    CHARLES
                (grinning, shaking his
                 head)
        Old lady finally dumped me. Took
        the kid, too.

                    CELL MATE
                (smirking)
        Didn't even know you had a kid.

                    CHARLES
                 (laughing)
          Yeah... neither did I.

Manson chuckles to himself, the laughter hollow, meaningless.
He stares at the ceiling, his mind already drifting
elsewhere—to his music, to his next move. To the next con,
the next trick. The past no longer mattered. His family,
his child—they were ghosts now, barely worth remembering.

The prison hums with the quiet murmurs of men locked away,
their lives etched into the walls. Manson exhales deeply,
then reaches for his guitar, strumming a few lazy chords.

INT. TERMINAL ISLAND PRISON - WARDEN'S OFFICE - DAY

INSERT CARD: MARCH 21, 1967

The room is stark, sterile. A large wooden desk separates
WARDEN HARRIS, a gruff but level-headed man, from Charles
Manson, now 32, his hair longer, his demeanor oddly calm. A
thick file labeled MANSON, CHARLES sits between them. The
warden flips through the pages, barely glancing up.

                    WARDEN HARRIS
                 (flatly)
          Your time's up, Manson. Ten years
          served. You're being released.

Manson shifts uncomfortably, rubbing his fingers together.
His voice is even but firm.

                    CHARLES
                 (low)
          I'd rather stay.

The warden finally looks up, studying Manson with mild
curiosity.

                    WARDEN HARRIS
                 (scoffs)
          That's a first. Most men can't
          wait to get out of here.

Manson leans forward slightly, his eyes sharp but unreadable.

                    CHARLES
                 (smirking)
          Out there, man... it ain't the
          same. Inside, I got a bed. A
          routine. I know how things work.

The warden exhales, shaking his head as he closes the file.

>   WARDEN HARRIS
>   (scoffing)
>   You're done, Manson. The state
>   doesn't keep men just 'cause they
>   don't wanna leave.

Manson knows arguing is useless. He forces a grin and stands
as the warden motions for the guard to escort him out.

EXT. TERMINAL ISLAND PRISON - FRONT GATES - DAY

A large metal gate groans open. Manson steps out, blinking
against the harsh California sun. The world outside is
unfamiliar—cars are sleeker, fashion has changed. The Summer
of Love is underway, and the world has moved on without him.

He looks left, then right. No one is waiting for him. No
family. No friends. He takes a deep breath and steps
forward into a new kind of freedom.

EXT. LOS ANGELES - NIGHT

Manson drifts through Los Angeles, a ghost in the sprawling
city. His first stops are among the Scientologists, a crowd
that seems to intrigue him. He attends parties for movie
stars, blending into the background, watching, listening. He
absorbs their mannerisms, their confidence, their ability to
command attention.

A Scientology auditor works with him, guiding him through 150
hours of auditing, probing deep into his thoughts, his fears,
his manipulations. Manson, always looking for an angle,
studies the techniques carefully, seeing how easily people
give up their secrets.

INT. PAYPHONE BOOTH - BERKELEY, CA - DAY (APRIL 1967)

Charles Manson leans casually against the glass of a
weathered payphone booth, cigarette dangling from his lips.
The street outside is alive with the pulse of the Haight-
Ashbury counterculture, but Manson stays focused, the phone
pressed to his ear. He exhales slowly as the line rings on
the other end.

INT. SAN FRANCISCO PROBATION OFFICE - ROGER SMITH'S DESK -
SAME TIME

FEDERAL PROBATION OFFICER ROGER SMITH, a sharp, methodical
man in his mid-40s, sits at his cluttered desk. His office
is lined with criminology textbooks and case files.

The phone buzzes, and he picks it up, flipping a probation
logbook open with his free hand.

                    ROGER SMITH
               (speaking briskly)
          San Francisco Probation Office,
          Officer Smith.

INTERCUT - PHONE CONVERSATION

                    CHARLES MANSON
               (smooth, almost cheerful)
          Hey now, this Roger Smith?

Smith's brow furrows as he reaches for a pen, sensing
something off.

                    ROGER SMITH
               (suspicious)
          Who's this?

                    CHARLES
               (chuckling)
          Name's Charlie. Charles Manson.
          Just got out, y'know?   Supposed to
          be in LA, but... figured I'd check
          in. See, I'm up in Berkeley now.

Smith immediately flips through Manson's file, his finger
tracing the release terms. His jaw tightens.

                    ROGER SMITH
               (serious)
          You're supposed to be in Los
          Angeles. Moving without
          authorization? That's a parole
          violation, Manson.

Manson inhales deeply, exhaling smoke into the receiver,
unbothered.

                    CHARLES
               (lazily)
          Yeah, I hear ya, but listen—LA
          ain't the place for me, man.
          Berkeley, though? Real groovy
          scene. Feels... right. Figured
          I'd do the right thing, call in,
          let you know where I'm at.

Smith leans back in his chair, glancing at research papers on
criminal behavior strewn across his desk. His initial
irritation shifts to curiosity.

He's been studying probation patterns—Manson is an anomaly, a wildcard. He drums his fingers on the desk, considering.

                    ROGER SMITH
               (slowly)
          You're lucky you made this call. I
          could have you hauled back for this
          stunt.

Manson smirks, sensing an opportunity.

                    CHARLES
               (smooth)
          But you won't.

Smith exhales, intrigued by the confidence. He closes Manson's file and grabs a new transfer form.

                    ROGER SMITH
               (after a pause)
          I'm transferring your case to my
          office. You report to me now.

Manson grins, flicking the cigarette butt onto the pavement, watching it smolder.

                    CHARLES
               (smirking)
          Knew you'd see it my way, boss.

Manson hangs up before Smith can say anything else. He steps out of the booth, stretching, one step closer to embedding himself in the heart of San Francisco's counterculture.

EXT. UNIVERSITY OF CALIFORNIA, BERKELEY - CAMPUS LIBRARY - DAY

Manson, now living on the streets, panhandles outside the UC Berkeley library. His charisma attracts attention, especially from MARY BRUNNER, a 23-year-old graduate of the University of Wisconsin-Madison. She notices him day after day, watching the way he charms people, the ease with which he moves through a crowd.

One evening, she finally speaks to him.

                    MARY
               (softly)
          You don't seem like most of the
          guys out here.

Manson grins, leaning against a tree.

                    CHARLES
                 (amused)
            That's 'cause I ain't.

A few conversations later, Manson's charm has worked its way
under her skin. She invites him to stay at her apartment,
offering him a couch, a little stability.

INT. MARY BRUNNER'S APARTMENT - NIGHT

The apartment is small but cozy—bookshelves stacked high, a
record player spinning soft jazz. Manson sprawls on the
couch, a cigarette between his fingers. Mary sits across
from him, intrigued, watching as he talks.

                    CHARLES
                 (low, hypnotic)
            Society, man, they just wanna
            control you. Make you follow their
            rules, their clocks, their laws.
            You ever think about breaking free?

Mary tilts her head, fascinated. She's never met anyone like
him. He speaks with such conviction, such authority. And
she likes the attention.

                    MARY
                 (hesitant)
            I don't know. I've always done
            what's expected of me.

Manson smirks, taking a long drag of his cigarette before
leaning forward.

                    CHARLES
                 (softly)
            Maybe it's time you stopped.

Mary bites her lip, considering. Manson leans back, knowing
he's planted the seed. Soon, she'll follow him anywhere.

EXT. SAN FRANCISCO - HAIGHT-ASHBURY - DAY

Manson walks through Haight-Ashbury, the counterculture
capital of the world. The air is thick with incense,
patchouli, and the distant strumming of acoustic guitars.
Hippies dance barefoot in the streets, poets read to small
crowds on the sidewalks, and LSD-fueled conversations swirl
through the air.

Manson watches it all, a small grin playing on his lips.
This—this is where he was meant to be.

The scene is ripe for someone like him. People are searching
for meaning, for belonging, for a leader. And he's about to
give them one.

EXT. BERKELEY CAMPUS - PARK BENCH - DAY (SUMMER 1967)

A warm afternoon sun filters through the tall eucalyptus
trees surrounding the University of California, Berkeley
campus. Students lounge on the grass, some strumming
guitars, others lost in conversation about revolution, love,
and psychedelics. The air is thick with the promise of
change.

Sitting alone on a bench, LYNETTE "SQUEAKY" FROMME, a freckle-
faced 19-year-old runaway, watches the world pass by. Her
red hair catches the sunlight, but there's a sadness in her
eyes—a loneliness. She tugs absentmindedly at a frayed
sleeve, her other hand clutching a well-worn copy of On the
Road by Jack Kerouac. She barely notices the lean figure who
slides onto the bench beside her.

                    CHARLES MANSON
               (soft, easygoing)
          You look like you been waiting for
          something.

Lynette startles, looking up. Charles Manson, his beard just
starting to grow in, his eyes dark and unreadable, watches
her with an almost disarming warmth. She tenses but doesn't
move away.

                    LYNETTE "SQUEAKY" FROMME
               (uncertain)
          I... I was just—

                    CHARLES
               (amused)
          Just what? Thinking? Wondering
          where you fit in all this?

She studies him, wary but intrigued. His voice is hypnotic,
filled with something that feels like understanding. Like he
sees through her.

                    LYNETTE "SQUEAKY" FROMME
               (softly)
          Maybe.

Manson leans in slightly, lowering his voice just enough to
pull her in closer.

                    CHARLES
                (low, sincere)
        Ain't nothing wrong with that, Red.
        Lotta folks out here looking for
        the same thing. You don't gotta
        figure it all out alone.

Something flickers in her eyes. No one's ever spoken to her
like this. No one's ever seen her like this.

INT. MARY BRUNNER'S APARTMENT - NIGHT

Mary Brunner stands with her arms crossed, her jaw tight as
she glares at Lynette, who sits on the couch next to Manson.
A single candle flickers, casting long shadows on the walls.
The place is cramped, the air thick with cigarette smoke.

                     MARY
                (flatly)
        Charlie, we talked about this.

Manson sits on the floor, playing a soft, bluesy tune on his
guitar, seemingly unfazed by Mary's frustration. Lynette
watches him, enthralled.

                    CHARLES
                (calm, reassuring)
        We did. And I told you, we ain't
        meant to be locked into rules,
        babe. Love don't work like that.

Mary exhales sharply, shaking her head. Manson looks up at
her, his voice lowering to a gentle, persuasive whisper.

                 CHARLES (CONT'D)
                (soft)
        You said you wanted to be free,
        didn't you? No chains. No walls.
        Just us.

Mary hesitates. His words dig into her, twisting her
emotions. Freedom. Love. Belonging. That's what he
promised her. She looks at Lynette, who stares back, hopeful
and lost all at once. After a long pause, Mary drops her
arms, her expression resigned.

Manson smiles, triumphant.

MONTAGE - THE FAMILY GROWS

EXT. HAIGHT-ASHBURY - DAY

Manson walks the streets of Haight-Ashbury, a place bursting
with life, music, and rebellion. He watches, observes,
targets the ones who seem adrift—young women with nowhere to
go, men who feel like outsiders.

INT. MARY'S APARTMENT - NIGHT

More women fill the space, their laughter echoing off the
walls. They sit cross-legged around Manson as he speaks in
low, poetic tones, his words weaving a new reality around
them.

EXT. GOLDEN GATE PARK - DAY

Manson strums his guitar as a group of followers sways around
him, hanging onto every note, every lyric. He isn't just
playing music—he's preaching.

INT. MARY'S APARTMENT - EVENING

Now the space is overflowing. Eighteen women fill the
apartment, some sitting on the floor, some curled up in
corners, all of them focused on him. Mary watches, no longer
resisting, her gaze locked onto Manson like the rest.

END MONTAGE.

EXT. HAIGHT-ASHBURY - NIGHT

The neighborhood is alive with the spirit of 1967's Summer of
Love. Manson, surrounded by a growing flock, walks among the
hippies and drifters, his voice a soft hum in the chaos.

                    CHARLES
               (low, preaching)
          See, man... we're the new
          Christians. And the world?
          They're the Romans. They just
          wanna crucify love, crucify
          freedom. But we ain't tied down by
          their rules. We're gonna show them
          what real life is.

A girl in the crowd nods eagerly, completely enraptured.
Others lean in closer, drawn to him. The air feels thick,
electric, as if a movement is being born right there in the
streets.

Manson smiles to himself. It's working. The Family is
growing.

EXT. TOPANGA CANYON - DIRT ROAD - DAY (LATE SUMMER 1967)

The old school bus rumbles down a winding dirt road, kicking
up clouds of dust. The seats inside have been ripped out,
replaced with vibrant rugs, mismatched pillows, and blankets.
The walls are covered in hand-painted symbols and psychedelic
patterns. Inside, Charles Manson sits cross-legged near the
front, strumming a worn guitar as the bus bounces along the
uneven terrain.

Around him, several women lounge, their bare feet resting on
the wood-paneled floor. Among them is Mary Brunner, visibly
pregnant, her hand resting on her belly. Lynette "Squeaky"
Fromme leans against the window, humming along to Manson's
melody. The bus is filled with laughter, smoke, and the hazy
aura of free-spirited abandon.

                    LYNETTE "SQUEAKY" FROMME
               (grinning)
          Charlie, where are we even going?

Manson flashes a mischievous grin, his fingers still plucking
at the guitar strings.

                    CHARLES
               (preaching)
          We ain't going nowhere, baby. And
          that's exactly where we need to be.

The others chuckle, nodding along as if his words carry a
divine weight. The bus continues winding through the
California landscape, the sun casting long shadows on the
road ahead.

EXT. LOS ANGELES - VENICE BEACH - NIGHT

Manson and his followers, now dubbed "The Family," roam the
Venice boardwalk, blending in with the hippies and drifters.
The salty breeze carries the sound of bongo drums, waves
crashing, and distant laughter.

Manson, now introducing himself as Charles Willis Manson,
weaves through the crowd, his charisma magnetic. A group of
young women, lost and searching, watch as he speaks in low,
rhythmic tones.

                    CHARLES
              (soft, persuasive)
     The world's got it all backwards,
     man. You gotta unlearn what they
     taught you. Out here? We make our
     own reality.

They nod eagerly, entranced. The Family is growing.

EXT. SPAHN RANCH - CALIFORNIA - DAY (SUMMER 1967)

The Spahn Movie Ranch is a sun-bleached, forgotten relic of
old Hollywood westerns. Deserted stables, dilapidated barns,
and abandoned buildings scatter the landscape. The air is
thick with dust and the scent of dry sagebrush.

Manson steps out of the school bus, surveying the land like a
prophet arriving in the promised land. Behind him, his
followers spill out, stretching their limbs, barefoot and
free.

                  MARY BRUNNER
              (wiping sweat from her
               brow)
     We're really staying here?

                    CHARLES
              (nods, smiling)
     Home sweet home, baby.

The elderly owner, GEORGE SPAHN, watches from a rocking chair
on the front porch. He's blind, but he knows something is
different about this group.

                 GEORGE SPAHN
              (gruffly)
     You folks planning to pay rent?

Manson steps forward, resting an arm on the old man's
shoulder like a long-lost friend.

                    CHARLES
              (smoothly)
     George, man... We ain't got money,
     but we got time. We got hands. We
     can take care of this place—fix up
     what needs fixing. And my girls?
     They'll keep you company.

Squeaky Fromme steps up, placing a gentle hand on George's
arm, her voice soft and saccharine.

                         LYNETTE "SQUEAKY" FROMME
                    (playfully)
               I'll make sure you're taken care
               of, Mr. Spahn.

Spahn grumbles but smirks, nodding slowly. The deal is made.
The Family has a new home.

INT. NORTH TEXAS STATE UNIVERSITY - DORM ROOM - DAY

INSERT CARD: DENTON, TEXAS 1967

The dorm room is small and cluttered. Posters of football
players and a calendar with exam dates line the walls. A
young, clean-cut CHARLES "TEX" WATSON, male white, 21, sits
at a desk strewn with textbooks, a half-eaten sandwich, and
unopened bills. His eyes are tired, his expression one of
quiet frustration. He stares at a tuition invoice, the red
"PAST DUE" stamp practically glowing on the page.

The faint sound of cheers comes from outside—a game is
playing on a radio down the hall—but Tex doesn't smile. He's
distracted.

                         TEX
                    (to himself)
               I need a break... something's
               gotta give.

He pushes away from the desk and walks across the room to a
phone mounted on the wall. He dials quickly.

                         TEX (CONT'D)
                    (into phone)
               Yeah, Braniff Airlines? You still
               hiring part-time?

INT. DALLAS LOVE FIELD - BRANIFF INTERNATIONAL - BAGGAGE AREA
- DAY

Tex, now wearing a Braniff International uniform, wrestles
with heavy suitcases on a busy airport tarmac. The sun is
hot, and the air buzzes with the sound of engines and radio
chatter. His movements are fast and practiced—he's been
working here for a few months now.

Inside the breakroom, Tex sits across from another baggage
handler, flipping through a worn Braniff travel privileges
handbook. A page offering free employee airline tickets is
circled in ink.

                    FELLOW HANDLER
                  (grinning)
          Man, you know you can fly anywhere
          with that? Long as you're on
          standby.

Tex nods slowly, wheels clearly turning in his head.

                    TEX
                  (smirking)
          I got a buddy out in L.A. Might be
          time to check out the coast.

EXT. LOS ANGELES - LAX AIRPORT - DAY

A Braniff plane touches down. Tex steps off the plane in
neatly pressed khakis, suitcase in hand, and a look of awe on
his face. Palm trees, smoggy sunlight, and the hum of city
traffic surround him as he exits the terminal.

Waiting by the curb is his fraternity brother, DAVID NEALE,
male white, 22, scruffier and more relaxed, wearing a
colorful button-down shirt and bell-bottom jeans.

                    DAVID
                  (grinning)
          Tex! Damn, look at you—still look
          like you walked off the cover of a
          church bulletin.

                    TEX
                  (grinning back)
          You look like you walked off a
          spaceship, man.

They laugh, then hug. David slaps Tex on the back and leads
him to a beat-up Volkswagen van.

INT. DAVID'S APARTMENT - WEST HOLLYWOOD - NIGHT

A dimly lit apartment filled with lava lamps, incense smoke,
and the sound of Jefferson Airplane playing from a turntable.
Posters of Jimi Hendrix and The Doors hang crookedly on the
walls. Young men and women lounge on bean bags and floor
cushions, passing around a joint, sipping wine, laughing
freely.

Tex sits stiffly at first, trying to process the scene. A
barefoot girl with long hair offers him the joint. He
hesitates... then takes it.

A few moments later, his posture relaxes. He listens as someone strums a guitar in the corner, and a girl dances in front of a psychedelic film loop projected on the wall. His eyes widen as he takes it all in—the music, the movement, the freedom.

>   TEX
>   (softly, to himself)
>   This... this is something else.

EXT. SUNSET STRIP - NIGHT

David and Tex walk along the bustling Sunset Strip, passing clubs like the Whisky a Go Go and the Roxy, the sidewalks packed with long-haired youth, street performers, poets, and acid-dropping runaways.

Music spills out of every doorway. Cars crawl through traffic, windows down, blasting The Byrds, The Doors, Janis Joplin. The entire world feels like it's vibrating on a different frequency.

>   DAVID
>   (shouting over the noise)
>   What do you think?

>   TEX
>   (stunned, eyes wide)
>   It's like another planet, man.

INT. DAVID'S APARTMENT - KITCHEN - MORNING

Tex sits at the breakfast table, a cup of coffee in one hand, flipping through a Los Angeles apartment guide with the other. His expression is focused, determined. David walks in, yawning.

>   DAVID
>   You flyin' back today?

Tex shakes his head slowly.

>   TEX
>   Nah. I'm thinkin' I'll stick
>   around a while. Something's
>   happenin' here... and I want to be
>   part of it.

MONTAGE - TEX'S TRANSFORMATION

Tex grows his hair longer, ditching the clean-cut look for sandals, denim, and paisley shirts.

He attends be-ins in Griffith Park, listens to gurus, plays bongos under trees.

He watches a girl swirl in a sun-drenched field, her face turned to the sky.

The smoggy skyline of Los Angeles becomes his new home.

END MONTAGE.

INT. CONDEMNED HOUSE - TOPANGA CANYON - NIGHT (APRIL 15, 1968)

A dimly lit, run-down house. The walls are cracked, the roof partially caved in, but the air is charged with anticipation. The room is filled with flickering candlelight, casting dancing shadows on the walls.

Mary Brunner lies on a makeshift bed of blankets and pillows, her breath ragged. Her face glistens with sweat, her fingers clutching the fabric beneath her. Around her, several young women from The Family kneel beside her, whispering soft words of encouragement.

Manson kneels beside her, his hands resting lightly on her swollen belly. His voice is soothing, hypnotic.

                    CHARLES
              (soft, reassuring)
          Breathe, Mother Mary. He's coming,
          just like he's supposed to.

Mary cries out, her body tensing as another wave of pain crashes over her. The women whisper prayers, rocking slightly in unison, as if part of a sacred ritual.

Finally—a small wail breaks through the air.

The women gasp in unison. Manson smiles, eyes locked onto the newborn child now resting in Mary's arms. His voice is hushed, reverent.

                    CHARLES (CONT'D)
              (whispering)
          Valentine Michael... Welcome to
          the world, little one.

The baby's cries fill the hollow house, a new life born into chaos. The women cry and laugh, rocking gently as they pass the child between them. Mary, exhausted but glowing, holds her son close.

Manson presses a hand to her forehead, like a preacher blessing his most devoted follower.

                    CHARLES (CONT'D)
               (gently)
          You're Mother Mary now. The world
          don't own you no more.

Mary smiles weakly, nodding. She belongs to something greater now. They all do. The Family is complete.

FLASHBACK:

INT. CALIFORNIA CORCORAN STATE PRISON - 1994

A grainy video recording flickers to life, its quality degraded like an old VHS tape played one too many times. The screen displays a faint time code in the corner, barely legible, jumping slightly every few seconds. The audio is murky, an eerie reverb distorting the words, making the voice sound as if it's trapped in an echo chamber.

INT. CALIFORNIA CORCORAN STATE PRISON - INTERVIEW ROOM - NIGHT

A dimly lit prison interview room, its walls dull and featureless. Charles Manson, age 60, sits shackled in a wooden chair, hands cuffed to a heavy chain that runs across his lap. His long, tangled hair falls around his lined face, a grizzled mustache and goatee framing his sharp features.

Two PRISON GUARDS stand motionless against the back wall, watching him closely. Their posture is rigid, their hands resting near their belts, ready for anything. The tension in the room is thick, but Manson himself is uncharacteristically subdued—a stark contrast to his usual manic energy in past interviews.

Manson's eyes dart around, scanning the room with an almost childlike curiosity, before settling forward. He leans back slightly in the chair, shifting against the unforgiving wooden slats, the chains at his waist clinking softly.

                    CHARLES
               (muttering, contemplative)
          Yeah, yeah... you know, I get
          around.

He pauses, blinking slowly as if sifting through decades of memories, his voice thick with nostalgia but devoid of enthusiasm. His posture is loose, his speech slightly disjointed, like a man reminiscing but unsure why it matters.

                    CHARLES (CONT'D)
               (low, casual)
          That's my neighborhood, you know.
          Like, uh... Jimi Hendrix
          lived—what? Three doors down from
          Dennis... and Elvis? Man, he was
          just a couple blocks over.

Manson tilts his head, as if picturing the streets of Los
Angeles, lost in a haze of half-remembered nights. He
chuckles lightly, but it lacks joy, the sound more of an
afterthought than genuine amusement.

                    CHARLES (CONT'D)
               (smirking)
          It's just like goin' lookin' in
          somebody else's icebox.

A soft static hums through the recording, the distortion
making his words almost otherworldly, as if his voice is
stretching across time.

Manson shifts again, glancing up toward the unseen
interviewer, his expression unreadable. His dark eyes gleam,
though whether it's from memory or something else entirely is
unclear.

                    CHARLES (CONT'D)
               (quiet, reflective)
          But see, here's the thing... me,
          in particular? I'm not... uh, you
          know, like...

He trails off, staring at something unseen. A few seconds of
dead air pass before he continues, his words slower now, more
deliberate.

                    CHARLES (CONT'D)
               (softly, shaking his head)
          I'm not impressed very easily. Not
          very much, you know.

He exhales through his nose, a long, measured breath. Then,
without warning, his lips twitch into a small grin—not his
usual wild grin, but something more subdued, almost self-
aware.

                    CHARLES (CONT'D)
               (amused)
          I'm impressed by my counselor and
          the associate warden, though.

Manson shifts in his chair, the chains rattling as he leans
forward ever so slightly, his eyes flashing with mischief.

                         CHARLES (CONT'D)
                     (chuckling, grinning)
              To see if I can get to... uh,
              uh... heh, heh, heh...

He lets the laugh trail off, low and strange, half-mocking,
half-genuine. His fingers twitch in the cuffs, and he tilts
his head, as if savoring the punchline of a joke only he
understands.

                         CHARLES (CONT'D)
                     (grinning, whispering)
              Get to a guitar.

The room is silent except for the faint hum of the tape
recording. The guards don't react, standing stone-faced.
The interviewer remains unseen, their presence barely
acknowledged. But Manson, for a brief moment, seems
genuinely lost in the thought of music, his fingers twitching
as if already strumming invisible chords.

A long pause, then—

END FLASHBACK.

EXT. PACIFIC COAST HIGHWAY - MALIBU, CALIFORNIA - AFTERNOON
(APRIL 6, 1968)

The sun hangs low in the sky, casting a golden hue over the
rolling waves of the Pacific Ocean. The Pacific Coast
Highway glimmers with heat waves. DENNIS WILSON, male white,
23, drummer of the Beach Boys, cruises in his red Ferrari 275
GTB, the engine purring as the wind rushes through his hair.

He's wearing a loose white button-up shirt, half-unbuttoned,
sleeves rolled to the elbows, and aviator sunglasses that
catch the light just right. Dennis drums his fingers on the
steering wheel in rhythm with the radio—"California Girls"
plays softly on the stereo.

As the car rounds a curve near Surfrider Beach, two young
women come into view—PATRICIA KRENWINKEL (female white, 20,
long dark hair, earth-toned clothes, eyes cast downward), and
ELLA JO BAILEY (female white, 19, blonde, barefoot, wearing a
fraying poncho and beads). They're standing on the shoulder,
their thumbs out, arms raised toward the traffic.

Dennis slows instinctively.

INT. FERRARI - CONTINUOUS

He sizes them up in the rearview as he approaches. Something
about them—dusty, lost, vulnerable—triggers his curiosity.
He pulls over with a soft screech of tires.

EXT. HIGHWAY SHOULDER - CONTINUOUS

The girls approach the car slowly, unsure. Dennis leans
across the passenger seat, grinning.

                    DENNIS WILSON
          Need a ride?

                    PATRICIA KRENWINKEL
                (small smile)
          Yeah. Thanks.

                    ELLA JO
          We're just headed a bit down the
          coast, near Las Flores.

Dennis unlocks the passenger door. The girls slide in,
Patricia in the front, Ella Jo climbing into the small
backseat, squatting with her knees hugged to her chest. The
inside of the car smells like cologne, salt air, and
marijuana.

INT. FERRARI - DRIVING - MOMENTS LATER

They drive along the coastline. The ocean rolls beside them
like a slow-moving dream. The air is filled with a
comfortable silence for a moment, then Dennis speaks.

                    DENNIS WILSON
          You two from around here?

                    ELLA JO
          Not really. We kind of go wherever
          the day takes us.

                    PATRICIA KRENWINKEL
                (quietly)
          We've been staying with some
          friends out in Topanga.

Dennis nods, glancing over at Patricia. She seems tired, a
bit spaced out, but there's something mysterious in her
silence. Ella Jo is a little more animated, soaking in the
drive like a tourist on a spiritual pilgrimage.

>   DENNIS WILSON
>   You ever surf?

>   PATRICIA KRENWINKEL
>   (shaking her head)
>   Just watch the water sometimes.

>   ELLA JO
>   Charlie says the ocean's got
>   secrets.

Dennis raises an eyebrow, intrigued.

>   DENNIS WILSON
>   Charlie?

>   ELLA JO
>   He's kind of... our teacher. He
>   plays music. Talks about love, the
>   Earth, you know... soul stuff.

Dennis laughs lightly.

>   DENNIS WILSON
>   Sounds like half the people I've
>   met this year.

They all share a short laugh, but Patricia's eyes remain distant, fixated on the shimmering waves.

EXT. LAS FLORES CANYON ROAD - DAY

Dennis slows the car and pulls over near a dusty dirt road leading inland toward Topanga Canyon. The girls begin to gather their things—small canvas bags, a rolled-up blanket.

>   PATRICIA KRENWINKEL
>   Thanks for the ride.

>   DENNIS WILSON
>   No problem. You girls be careful
>   out here, alright?

Ella Jo leans on the car door for a second, flashing him a serene, almost grateful smile.

>   ELLA JO
>   Charlie would like you. You've got
>   good energy.

Patricia nods vaguely, and the two girls begin walking up the dirt road, disappearing into the brush-lined path like two spirits slipping into another realm.

Dennis watches them go for a beat, unsettled but curious. He shakes his head, pulls back onto the highway, and drives off—unaware that this brief encounter is just the first ripple in a tidal wave of chaos that will change his life.

INT. HAIGHT ASHBURY FREE MEDICAL CLINIC (HAFMC) - SAN FRANCISCO - SPRING 1968

A cramped, dimly lit waiting room filled with young people—hippies, runaways, addicts, all seeking medical care or a warm place to rest. Posters promoting "Free Love" and "Turn on, Tune in, Drop out" cover the peeling walls. The scent of incense and sweat lingers in the air.

Roger Smith, a federal probation officer and researcher, sits behind a desk cluttered with medical reports and research notes. He adjusts his glasses as he watches Charles Manson, who lounges in a chair across from him, legs stretched out, barefoot and smiling.

Manson's hair is longer now, unkempt but intentional, his beard beginning to take shape. His eyes dart around the room, hyper-aware of his surroundings, like a predator assessing his environment.*

INT. HAFMC - ROGER SMITH'S OFFICE - DAY

Smith flips through Manson's file, clicking his pen against the desk, eyeing the man in front of him with cautious intrigue.

                    ROGER SMITH
               (skeptical)
          So you want to move from Berkeley
          to Haight-Ashbury?

Manson nods, his grin widening.

                    CHARLES
          Man, you ever been out there? It's
          electric. This whole city's
          changing—Haight's where it's
          happening.

Smith leans back, tapping his fingers against the desk.

                    ROGER SMITH
          You're still under federal
          supervision, Charlie. Moving
          around ain't exactly encouraged.

                    CHARLES
                  (smirking)
          But you can make it happen, can't
          ya?

Smith studies Manson for a beat. He knows letting him
integrate into the Haight-Ashbury scene could serve his
research into counterculture behavior. After a pause, he
sighs and scribbles a note on the file.

                    ROGER SMITH
          Alright. You're approved. Just
          don't disappear on me.

Manson beams, leaning forward, his hands clasped together
like a man receiving a divine blessing.

                    CHARLES
          I ain't goin' nowhere, boss.

EXT. HAIGHT-ASHBURY - GOLDEN GATE PARK - DAY

A kaleidoscope of counterculture—tie-dye-clad youth pass
joints and lounge in patches of sunlight. A group of folk
musicians strums on battered guitars as bongo drums thump
nearby.

Manson sits cross-legged beneath a massive eucalyptus tree,
surrounded by a small group of wide-eyed followers. His
voice is smooth, hypnotic, each word deliberate, calculated.

                    CHARLES
                  (softly)
          They been lying to you, man. The
          system, the Establishment. They
          make you think you need jobs,
          money, rules. But we ain't part of
          that world, are we?

A few heads shake, mesmerized. Lynette "Squeaky" Fromme,
sitting close, watches him with rapt attention.

Manson holds up a small tab of LSD, the paper square pinched
between his fingers.

                    CHARLES (CONT'D)
          This, man... This is freedom.
          This is truth.

He places the LSD on his tongue, closing his eyes as the drug
dissolves into his bloodstream. The others hesitate, then
follow his lead. The world tilts, colors shift. The wind
whispers secrets only they can hear.

Manson opens his eyes, his pupils now blown wide, his expression one of revelation. His voice drops into something more commanding.

                    CHARLES (CONT'D)
          We ain't just people, man. We're
          the new messiahs. They don't want
          us to know that—but I see it.

Squeaky leans in, her breath shallow.

                    LYNETTE "SQUEAKY" FROMME
               (low, in awe)
          What do you mean?

Manson grins, eyes burning with drug-fueled enlightenment.

                    CHARLES
          We're the real Christians, babe.
          This world? It's Rome, man. And
          Rome's gonna fall.

The group nods in agreement, their minds bending to his words. A new doctrine is forming, right here in the park, under the influence of LSD, rebellion, and unchecked charisma.

INT. HAFMC - DAVID SMITH'S LAB - NIGHT

Stacks of scientific reports, a whiteboard covered in scribbled chemical equations. DR. DAVID SMITH, male white, 28, the founder of the clinic, sits across from Roger Smith, reviewing research data on LSD and amphetamines. A manila folder labeled "Manson - Subject 437" rests between them.

                    DAVID SMITH
               (reading)
          His personality shift is the most
          abrupt I've ever seen. You've
          noticed it too, haven't you?

                    ROGER SMITH
               (nodding)
          Yeah. A year ago, he was just a
          petty conman. Now? He's out there
          preaching like a damn prophet.

                    DAVID SMITH
               (skeptical)
          It's the LSD. His brain
          chemistry's completely rewired.

Roger flips through a log of interactions with Manson's followers, his expression darkening.

                    ROGER SMITH
          And they worship him.

A long silence. They both know what's happening. They just don't know how far it will go.

INT. COMMUNE - NIGHT

A candle-lit room, walls lined with books—the Bible, Dale Carnegie's How to Win Friends and Influence People, and Robert Heinlein's Stranger in a Strange Land. Manson flips through the pages, murmuring to himself.

                    CHARLES
               (whispering)
          Thou art God... we are all God...

Squeaky and Mary Brunner sit nearby, listening. Manson slams the book shut, looking up, his eyes wild.

                    CHARLES (CONT'D)
          That's what the world don't
          understand. God ain't up there,
          man. God's inside us.

Brunner nods, deeply moved.

                    MARY BRUNNER
               (sincerely)
          That's... beautiful, Charlie.

Manson grins, seeing how deeply his words land. He steps forward, voice growing more urgent, more inspired.

                    CHARLES
          Think about it—the Romans crucified
          Christ, right? But Christ? He
          didn't die. He just... changed.
          And we? We're his new disciples.
          The world's still Rome, and Rome
          still don't want us free.

His followers nod, entranced. Squeaky whispers, almost to herself—

                    LYNETTE "SQUEAKY" FROMME
               (softly)
          We're the new Christians...

Manson's smile widens.

                    CHARLES
          Damn right.

EXT. HAIGHT-ASHBURY - SUNSET

Manson, now fully transformed, walks through the streets of
Haight-Ashbury, barefoot, untamed, magnetic. His following
grows daily, young men and women flocking to his words like
moths to a flame.

He preaches on street corners, his voice rising over the hum
of drums and guitar riffs.

                    CHARLES
               (shouting)
          Rome is gonna fall, man! And we're
          the ones who'll be left standing!

A few onlookers cheer, others stare, mesmerized. A movement
is forming. A cult is being born.

And no one—not the researchers, not the doctors, not even
Manson himself—realizes just how far it's going to go.

EXT. PACIFIC COAST HIGHWAY - MALIBU - DUSK (APRIL 11, 1968)

The sun dips low, casting orange and purple hues over the
rolling Pacific waves. The coastal air is thick with salt
and gasoline, the rhythmic whoosh of passing cars filling the
highway. Dennis Wilson speeds down the road in his red
Ferrari, radio humming a soft Beach Boys melody as he drives,
his mind elsewhere.

Then—two figures on the roadside.

The same two girls from earlier, Patricia Krenwinkel and Ella
Jo Bailey, stand hitchhiking, their faces lit by the last
light of day. This time, Dennis doesn't hesitate. He pulls
over, the car door swinging open.

                    DENNIS WILSON
               (grinning)
          Well, look at that. Guess the
          universe wanted us to meet again.

                    ELLA JO
               (laughing)
          Or maybe you just like picking up
          pretty girls.

Patricia smirks, brushing a strand of hair behind her ear.
They slide into the car—Patricia in the passenger seat, Ella
Jo in the back—barefoot, sun-kissed, carrying the scent of
dust and patchouli.

INT. WILSON'S SUNSET BOULEVARD HOME - NIGHT

Wilson's lavish home at 14400 Sunset Boulevard is a sprawling
Spanish-style estate, nestled in the hills, swimming pool
shimmering under the moonlight. The girls wander inside,
eyes wide at the sheer luxury—plush furniture, gold records
on the walls, the scent of weed and expensive cologne.

Dennis pours three glasses of wine, settling onto the couch
with the girls, his shirt unbuttoned, barefoot and relaxed.

                    DENNIS WILSON
              So, tell me—what's your story?
              Where are two free-spirited girls
              like you from?

                    PATRICIA KRENWINKEL
                 (leaning in)
              We don't really have a home. We've
              been living in Topanga with... our
              family.

                    DENNIS WILSON
                 (grinning)
              You mean hippies.

                    ELLA JO
                 (laughing)
              Something like that.

                    DENNIS WILSON
              And what? Just drifting around,
              picking up wisdom wherever you can?

The girls exchange a look. A secret understanding.

                    PATRICIA KRENWINKEL
              We've got a guru. Someone who sees
              things the rest of the world
              doesn't.

Wilson smirks, intrigued, but amused.

                    DENNIS WILSON
              Oh yeah? What kind of guru?

                    ELLA JO
              A real one. Charlie Manson.

A name that, in that moment, means nothing to him.

Dennis just chuckles, refilling his glass.

>   DENNIS WILSON
>   Yeah? Well, I spent some time with
>   a guru myself. The Maharishi
>   Mahesh Yogi. Taught me all about
>   meditation, energy, the universe.

The girls smile knowingly.

>   PATRICIA KRENWINKEL
>   That's good, Dennis. You're
>   already on the path.

Dennis smirks at the mystical undertone in her voice. He
finishes his drink, leans back, and the night drifts into
something else—candlelight flickering, bodies intertwined,
the air thick with incense and whispered philosophies.

INT. DENNIS WILSON'S HOME - MASTER BEDROOM - NIGHT

The master bedroom glows in soft amber light from the shaded
lamps.

Dennis Wilson lies on a wide, low-set bed, the sheets tousled
and half-draped. Patricia Krenwinkel and Ella Jo Bailey are
with him—both barefoot, wearing flowing skirts and loose tops
now slipping away in soft movements. The atmosphere is not
rushed; it's languid and dreamlike.

Their bodies move together, a tangle of limbs and shifting
shadows, illuminated by the flicker of candlelight and the
reflected shimmer from the pool outside. On the record
player in the corner, a slow, soulful track spins on
vinyl—raw and melancholic. Time seems to stretch, melt, then
dissolve.

There's a strange silence between them, not awkward, but
filled with something deeper: curiosity, disconnection,
longing. For the girls, it's transactional but also
spiritual—a ritual of bonding, of offering. For Dennis, it's
pleasure tinged with loneliness, curiosity tangled with
indulgence.

Outside the bedroom door, the rest of the house remains
quiet. But already, unseen, change is beginning. A presence
is drawing near

INT. RECORDING STUDIO - LATER THAT NIGHT

Dennis stands at a mixing console, wearing headphones, deep
in concentration. A Beach Boys session is underway,
instruments stacked, reels spinning. But his mind isn't
fully there. His thoughts flicker back to the two girls, to
their strange certainty, their talk of a guru. He shakes it
off, laughing to himself.

                    DENNIS WILSON
               (muttering)
          Charlie Manson... some hippie
          messiah.

He lets the thought fade, turning back to the music.

EXT. WILSON'S SUNSET BOULEVARD HOME - NIGHT

Dennis pulls into his driveway, headlights illuminating
something out of place—a massive black school bus parked in
front of his home, its sides covered in strange, hand-painted
symbols.

His brow furrows.

                    DENNIS WILSON
          What the hell?

As he gets out of the car, a small, wiry figure steps out of
the shadows. Long tangled hair, piercing eyes, a disarming
grin. Barefoot, dressed in ragged, loose clothing. The man
drops to his knees before Wilson and, in an unexpected
display, kisses his feet.

Dennis freezes.

The man looks up at him, smiling wide—Charles Manson.

                    CHARLES
               (low, warm)
          Hello, brother.

Dennis blinks, caught between amusement and unease.

                    DENNIS WILSON
               (raising an eyebrow)
          And who the hell might you be?

Manson rises slowly, hands extended in a peaceful gesture.

                    CHARLES
          Charlie. Your girls told me you
          were ready to meet the Family.

INT. WILSON'S HOME - MOMENTS LATER

Dennis steps inside—and freezes.

His house is full of people. At least a dozen—mostly young
women, draped in flowing skirts, barefoot, laughing softly,
moving as if they belong there. The scent of marijuana and
incense hangs in the air. The record player spins—some old
blues record, slow and hypnotic. A girl sits cross-legged on
the carpet, staring into a candle flame as if seeing a
vision.

Manson follows Dennis inside, moving with a slow, almost
theatrical grace.

                    DENNIS WILSON
                 (deadpan)
            Well, this is new.

Manson laughs, spreading his arms wide, as if presenting a
great gift.

                    CHARLES MANSON
            Brother... this is love.

MONTAGE - THE NEVER-ENDING PARTY

Dennis and Manson sit by the pool, deep in conversation.
Manson speaks in poetic riddles, hands weaving shapes in the
air, Dennis nodding along, sipping whiskey.

The girls bathe in the Jacuzzi, their laughter echoing
through the canyon.

Music plays nonstop—Manson strums Dennis' guitars, humming
melodies that feel improvised, yet hypnotic.

Wilson, mesmerized, listens as Manson preaches, eyes burning
with a prophet's fire.

Naked bodies dance under moonlight, a psychedelic fever
dream, a never-ending hedonistic commune.

END MONTAGE.

INT. WILSON'S BEDROOM - LATE NIGHT

Dennis stares at the ceiling, fully awake, as Manson's voice
echoes in his mind.

                    CHARLES (V.O.)
          We're not separate from the
          universe, man. We are the
          universe. No past. No future.
          Just now.

Dennis exhales, eyes flicking toward the open door of his
bedroom. Through the dim candlelight, he can see Manson,
sitting in the hallway, staring at him.

Not speaking. Not moving. Just watching.

Dennis swallows hard, the weight of something unspoken
settling over him.

EXT. CALIFORNIA STATE UNIVERSITY, LOS ANGELES - CAMPUS QUAD -
DAY (SPRING 1968)

Tex Watson, now 22, strolls through the sunny Cal State LA
campus. He wears a collared shirt, pressed slacks, and dark
sunglasses—still clinging to the clean-cut image of the young
man who'd once been a standout in his Texas hometown. But
his steps are slower now, less purposeful. He no longer
feels tethered to lectures, grades, or a future carved from
someone else's blueprint.

His textbooks are barely touched. His attention drifts
during lectures. The call of the city beyond the classroom
walls grows louder every day.

INT. LOS ANGELES WIG SHOP - WEST HOLLYWOOD - DAY

Tex works behind the counter of a modest wig shop off
Melrose, shelves lined with synthetic hairpieces and
mannequins with painted smiles. He's grown his hair out.
His shirts are looser, more colorful. He jokes with
customers, easygoing and charming.

In the backroom, he laughs with his fraternity brother, David
Neale, whom he helped land a job here. The work is light,
the money decent, and the nights? Full of possibility.

EXT. SUNSET BOULEVARD - LATE AFTERNOON

One warm day after work, Tex cruises down Sunset Boulevard in
his battered Chevy, windows down, letting the wind tug at his
shirt. The strip is alive with movement—hitchhikers,
musicians, barefoot girls weaving through traffic.

Up ahead, a man with sun-streaked blond hair, shirt open, thumb in the air. Tex pulls over instinctively. Picking up hitchhikers is part of the culture now.

The man slides into the passenger seat, sweat glistening on his forehead.

                    DENNIS WILSON
            (casual)
      Appreciate the ride, man.

They drive in silence for a moment before Tex asks the man's name.

                    DENNIS WILSON (CONT'D)
            (chuckling)
      Dennis. Dennis Wilson.

Tex nods politely. The name doesn't register.

                    DENNIS WILSON (CONT'D)
      Beach Boys.

That registers.

Tex glances over, eyes widening.

                    TEX
      For real?

Dennis grins and nods. He gives Tex an address — 14400 Sunset Boulevard.

EXT. 14400 SUNSET BOULEVARD - EARLY EVENING

The car rolls up to an enormous Spanish-style mansion nestled in the Palisades. White stucco, red-tiled roof, and lush greenery frame the house like a postcard.

Tex puts the car in park, jaw slightly slack. This isn't anything like the world he knows. His modest Texas upbringing feels a million miles away.

                    DENNIS WILSON
      You wanna come in for a drink?

Tex hesitates—then nods. He follows Dennis up the long driveway.

INT. DENNIS WILSON'S HOUSE - LIVING ROOM - MOMENTS LATER

The door swings open to reveal a surreal scene: a man with long, dark hair and intense eyes sits cross-legged on the floor, softly strumming a guitar. Around him, five or six young women in loose dresses and bare feet lie draped across pillows and woven blankets, laughing softly, swaying to the sound of the music.

The man doesn't look up, just keeps playing—soft, bluesy, hypnotic.

The mood is slow, sensual. The air carries the scent of sandalwood, marijuana, and ocean mist.

Tex freezes at the threshold.

There's something about the man on the floor—his stillness, his gravity. A presence that pulls the air inward.

A HOUSEGUEST nearby gestures to Tex.

> HOUSEGUEST
> (quietly)
> That's Charlie. Charlie Manson.

INT. DENNIS WILSON'S HOUSE - LIVING ROOM - LATER

Tex lingers in the corner of the room, unsure but fascinated. He watches Manson, who murmurs about love, freedom, acceptance—not in a preachy way, but with an offbeat rhythm, like poetry disguised as conversation.

The girls hang on his every word. They smile at Tex, welcoming him in with soft glances and gentle touches on the arm.

Something stirs in Tex—something aching and buried. A longing he didn't know he had.

His family back in Texas loved him, sure. But their love came with expectations, standards, moral rules. What he feels here is different: a kind of unconditional, judgment-free attention. No one asks what school he goes to, what church he belongs to, or what job he has.

For the first time, he feels seen—not as a student, a Texan, or a son—but just as himself.

He watches Charlie lean in, speaking softly to one of the girls. She closes her eyes and smiles.

It's not just the man. It's the atmosphere, the freedom, the slow pulse of something ancient and seductive.

Tex leans back into a cushion, exhales, and lets it wash over him.

MONTAGE - TEX'S SUMMER AT DENNIS WILSON'S HOUSE

Tex sprawls beside the pool, a girl resting her head on his shoulder.

He shares joints, strums guitars, helps Charlie fix a broken van.

He listens to Manson speak by firelight, lost in the rhythm of his voice.

He helps cook, sings with the group, and begins to let go of his old self.

END MONTAGE.

EXT. SPAHN RANCH - DAY (WEEKS LATER)

The transition is almost seamless. Soon, Tex is no longer a guest.

He's a follower.

INT. DENNIS WILSON'S HOUSE - LIVING ROOM - DAY

Charles Manson lounges in the center of the room like a prophet at rest, cross-legged on the shag carpet, guitar across his lap, plucking out slow, hypnotic chords. Around him, dozens of young women move in and out of rooms, carrying baskets of fruit, rolling joints, massaging shoulders, cleaning surfaces, and occasionally dancing in slow, sensual movements.

Tex Watson stands in the corner, watching. His expression is part awe, part disbelief. He no longer wears the starched button-downs or polished loafers of his college days. He's barefoot, sun-kissed, his hair growing wild, his jeans frayed at the hem.

Across the room, Manson catches his eye—offers a knowing smile, a nod that says, You're here now. You're one of us.

EXT. BACKYARD - LATER

Tex sits by the pool with a worn duffel bag in front of him.
One by one, he pulls out the last remnants of his old life:

A gold wristwatch

A wallet filled with IDs and cards

A pair of polished boots

Keys to his car

A shirt from college

He pauses, running his fingers over each item, letting
memories flicker and fade. Then he gathers everything into a
pile, walks barefoot to Manson—who is resting beneath a
jacaranda tree, eyes half-closed—and places it all at his
feet.

No words. No hesitation.

Manson looks up, doesn't touch the items, just smiles gently
and says nothing. Tex nods, and walks away lighter, as if
he's shed not just objects, but a former identity.

INT. DENNIS WILSON'S HOUSE - EVENING

Dennis moves through his home, glass of wine in hand, the sun
setting through the wide windows. He passes through rooms
that were once quiet, solitary spaces now filled with the
sounds of life and madness—music, dancing, whispered
conversations about cosmic vibrations, reincarnation, and the
coming revolution.

Manson sits on a couch in the center of it all, surrounded by
his women. He looks up at Dennis, grins.

Dennis Wilson, for all his success and celebrity, is
enchanted. He's never seen someone with such powerful calm,
someone who can take control of a room without raising his
voice. He begins calling Manson "the Wizard", referring to
him in conversations with friends like a mystic guide.

Manson rewards this trust with a performance of serenity,
charisma, and spiritual depth, even as his followers scrub
Wilson's floors, prepare his meals, and bathe him like a
prince.

MONTAGE - THE SIX-MONTH ARRANGEMENT

The Manson Family occupies the guest rooms and pool house, sleeping on floors, sharing mattresses, forming a constant commune within the mansion.

Dennis and Charlie sit by the pool late into the night, talking about esoteric philosophy, God, the universe, music, and death.

Girls bathe Dennis, brush his hair, and sing softly as Manson watches with quiet satisfaction.

Tex Watson carries supplies, follows orders, and listens to Manson's every word like gospel. He smiles more. Laughs more. Feels reborn.

The mansion becomes a haven for free love, LSD trips, and strange rituals, all under the seemingly peaceful, mesmerizing guidance of Charlie.

END MONTAGE.

INT. TEX WATSON'S ROOM - NIGHT

Tex lies back on a thin mattress on the floor, a breeze drifting through the open windows. One of the girls lies beside him, asleep. He stares at the ceiling, eyes wide, smiling faintly.

                    TEX (V.O.)
          "For years I'd struggled to
          accumulate all I could: the right
          car, the right clothes, the right
          things that would somehow complete
          what I thought was missing inside
          me... Now I gave all, everything I
          had, to Charlie. Suddenly I felt
          very free."

And somewhere, outside the bounds of this world of illusion and ecstasy, reality waits.

But inside Dennis Wilson's mansion?

The Family has taken root.

EXT. 14400 SUNSET BOULEVARD - DAY - LATE SUMMER 1968

The Manson Family's presence at Dennis Wilson's mansion had grown from unusual to full-scale occupation.

The poolside gatherings were daily rituals, filled with strumming guitars, dancing, and hypnotic monologues from Charlie. Dennis, enthralled by the mystical air around Manson, found himself captivated—not just by Charlie's charisma, but by his music.

Manson often carried his beat-up acoustic guitar, strumming meditative melodies, murmuring lyrics that drifted between peace and foreboding. His songs weren't polished, but they were raw, haunting, urgent—a blend of blues, folk, and incantation. They caught Dennis's ear in a way that few things had.

INT. BRIAN WILSON'S HOME STUDIO - NIGHT

Inside the private home studio of Beach Boys co-founder Brian Wilson, a sacred place of creativity and experimentation, Charles Manson stands in front of a microphone. He's barefoot, eyes half-closed, swaying as he strums slowly. Behind the control panel, STEPHEN DESPER, male white, 26, the band's engineer, keeps the levels steady, watching the unorthodox session unfold.

In the booth, Dennis Wilson sits beside TERRY MELCHER, male white, 28, the successful producer best known for his work with The Byrds, observing curiously.

Manson's voice floats into the mic—low, droning, filled with both sweetness and menace. The songs are vague in structure, but dense with strange, spiritual metaphors and veiled threats wrapped in love-language. They aren't commercial, but they're impossible to ignore.

                    STEPHEN DESPER (V.O.)
          Those recordings... they weren't
          for an album. They were for Dennis
          and Terry. Something more
          personal. Like they were
          entertaining a prophet. Or toying
          with fire.

None of these recordings were ever publicly released. The tapes vanished—perhaps shelved, destroyed, or hidden.

INT. WESTERN RECORDING STUDIO - DAY - SEPTEMBER 1968

Meanwhile, Dennis, still fascinated by Manson's work, selects one of Charlie's songs—"Cease to Exist"—to record with the Beach Boys. He reworks the arrangement, changes the lyrics, and retitles it: "Never Learn Not to Love."

In the studio, the Beach Boys rehearse the track with professional sheen, smoothing out the chaotic sincerity of Manson's original. Charlie isn't present. His song is molded, edited, commercialized—stripped of its original tone.

INT. 14400 SUNSET BOULEVARD - NIGHT

Later that week, Manson confronts Dennis. The family is gone from the main room; it's just the two of them under the dim glow of antique sconces.

Manson's voice is low, dangerously calm.

                    CHARLES
          Why's my name not on that record?

Dennis, visibly tense, tries to explain.

                    DENNIS WILSON
          You gave it to me, Charlie. Said
          you didn't care about the money.
          You got a hundred thousand dollars'
          worth of food, cars,
          instruments—everything.

Charlie doesn't respond. Just stares.

The moment lingers, heavy with unspoken warning.

EXT. WILSON'S DRIVEWAY - DAYS LATER

Two of Dennis's luxury cars, including a Rolls-Royce, sit idle in the driveway. Family members—stoned, giggling—vandalize them with keys, rocks, and boot heels, as if performing some twisted liberation ritual.

The cars are trashed, the leather interiors ripped apart. Manson doesn't stop them. He watches quietly from the steps, smiling faintly.

INT. WILSON'S MANSION - LIVING ROOM - EARLY OCTOBER

The energy has shifted.

Dennis has grown increasingly disturbed by Manson's erratic behavior, the increasing drug use, the paranoia whispering at the edges of every gathering. He's begun sleeping at hotels, finding any excuse to stay away.

One morning, he simply doesn't return.

Within days, Dennis officially moves out, leasing a basement apartment in Santa Monica. He leaves the Family behind at the Sunset mansion—a retreat turned commune, now suffocating under the weight of delusion.

INT. SUNSET MANSION - BEDROOM - WEEKS LATER

The house is decaying.

Furniture is missing. Rooms that were once filled with light and laughter now echo with the mutterings of worn-out followers. Walls are marked with symbols, graffiti, and candle wax drippings. The Family has pillaged the home, stripping it of valuables, art, electronics, even cutlery.

Three weeks before the lease is due to expire, they are evicted by force.

INT. SANTA MONICA BASEMENT APARTMENT - DAY

A housekeeper opens the door to Dennis Wilson's new residence. She finds a bullet placed carefully on the entry table.

No note. Just a message.

Left by one of Manson's followers. Meant to be delivered to Dennis.

A promise.

A threat.

A signal that Charlie hadn't forgotten.

EXT. SANTA MONICA - BEACH - SUNSET

Dennis walks alone along the surf, shoes in hand, the tide licking at his ankles. He's haunted, no longer smiling. His time with Manson—once an adventure wrapped in spirituality and music—has unraveled into something dark, dangerous, and irreversible.

He watches the sun sink into the ocean, the rhythm of the waves no longer soothing.

Behind him, a shadow of regret stretches into the distance.

EXT. BARKER RANCH - PANAMINT RANGE, DEATH VALLEY - NOVEMBER 1968

The desert stretches endlessly, dust and jagged red rock dominating the horizon. Against this harsh landscape sits Barker Ranch—a modest compound of weathered wooden shacks nestled deep in the Panamint Mountains, surrounded by the wind-scoured silence of Death Valley.

The Spahn Ranch, once vibrant with movement and Manson's teachings, had fallen into disrepair—its structures decaying, crawling with tension, eyes of law enforcement starting to drift their way.

But Barker Ranch? It was isolated, better maintained, and forgotten by time.

INT. BARKER RANCH - MAIN CABIN - DAY

Inside the main cabin, a fire crackles in a stone hearth. Charles Manson paces slowly, barefoot on creaking floorboards. His eyes are alight with something new, something wilder than before.

The Beatles' White Album spins on a portable record player in the corner, the stylus crackling as "Helter Skelter" begins its chaotic descent into feedback and scream.

Manson stops pacing. He kneels beside the turntable, eyes locked on the spinning vinyl like it's a sacred relic.

Around him, the Family—dozens of young women and a few men—sit cross-legged, waiting. Listening.

EXT. DESERT MINESHAFT - TWILIGHT

A rusted mine shaft, its entrance half-buried in the sand, yawns like a forgotten wound in the earth.

Manson stands before it, arms outstretched, preaching to the faithful.

                    CHARLES (V.O.)
          They're talking to us. The
          Beatles. They know. The album is
          the prophecy. 'Helter
          Skelter'—that's the coming storm.

He declares that "Helter Skelter" is not just a song, but a coded message—a warning of the race war that's coming.

In Manson's twisted vision, the Black population will rise against the oppressive white system, but will falter at the moment of victory, unable to lead. That's when Manson and his Family—hidden away in an underground city beneath the desert, safe inside this mine—will emerge, clean, chosen, and divine.

INT. BARKER RANCH - NIGHT

The cabin is dark except for the firelight flickering against dusty window panes. Manson whispers to his inner circle—SUSAN ATKINS, 21, Patricia Krenwinkel, LESLIE VAN HOUTEN, 20, and others—feeding them visions of chaos and rebirth, stoking paranoia and apocalyptic fervor.

He speaks of "the pit", the place underground where they'll be safe.

He speaks of black uprising, of white annihilation, of a kingdom they will inherit.

The women listen, faces glowing with religious awe, their identities dissolving into his narrative.

MONTAGE - THE PREPARATION FOR "HELTER SKELTER"

Manson and Family members hike through the desert, searching for deeper mineshafts, mapping what they believe is an underground sanctuary.

Walls of the cabin become painted with symbols, coded messages from The Beatles. One reads: "Healter Skelter", misspelled but emphasized.

Weapons are cleaned and hidden. Food is hoarded. The Family becomes a survivalist cult wrapped in a psychedelic delusion.

Manson plays "Piggies" and "Blackbird" on repeat, claiming the Beatles are speaking directly to them.

Manson declares he will soon ignite the race war himself if the world refuses to recognize the prophecy.

END MONTAGE.

INT. HOLLYWOOD APARTMENT - DECEMBER 1968

Tex Watson, now separated from the Family, lies sprawled on a mattress in a dingy apartment with a new girlfriend, a petite brunette with sharp eyes and a streetwise air. She sells small quantities of LSD and marijuana, mostly to friends and passing strangers.

The apartment is cluttered with ashtrays, incense burners, and torn Rolling Stone magazines. The couple lives fast—partying, selling, floating from one high to the next.

Tex seems, at first, happier—sleeping late, waking up to someone who doesn't preach apocalypse. They make love, get stoned, laugh at the absurdity of it all.

But the feeling doesn't last.

In the quiet moments, Tex begins to feel a void again. Something spiritual is missing. Something terrifying and strange, but strangely comforting—the presence of Charlie, the sisterhood of the women, the sense of destiny he'd once felt at Spahn Ranch and Barker.

EXT. DESERT ROAD - DUSK (WEEKS LATER)

A beat-up car winds its way through the vast nothingness of the California desert. Behind the wheel: Tex Watson. Hair longer now, mustache growing in. His eyes squint toward the horizon.

He's going back.

Back to Manson.

Back to Barker Ranch.

Back to the place where Helter Skelter is waiting to begin.

FLASHBACK:

INT. CALIFORNIA CORCORAN STATE PRISON - INTERVIEW ROOM - NIGHT - 1994

A grainy VHS recording flickers to life, timestamped the bottom, glitching intermittently like an old surveillance tape. The frame is static, washed in green tones, with occasional scan lines distorting the image. The audio buzzes with reverb, voices bouncing off cold cement walls.

In the center of the frame, Charles Manson, 60, sits shackled and handcuffed in a straight-backed wooden chair, the metal restraints looped tightly around his waist and wrists. His hair is long and wiry, a tangled curtain framing his heavily lined face. A coarse beard and mustache give him the look of a man carved from stone.

He coughs—harsh and ugly, bending forward slightly as if the force of it shakes something loose from deep inside.

Then, slowly, he straightens. His eyes narrow. His voice
rises like a fog from the pit of his chest.

He looks toward someone off camera, the unseen presence
prompting his winding monologue.

                    CHARLES
          Yeah... yeah, I was in prison when
          Dianetics first started... 1950.
          We fought the establishment, man.

He scratches the side of his neck with his cuffed hand, an
almost involuntary tic.

                    CHARLES (CONT'D)
          The Black Muslims came in, man,
          they brought the Koran... the dark
          side of the moon stuff. The
          Islamic... ah... arm of the
          church. And then the Masons, too,
          that whole layer, y'know? I ain't
          even sure how deep that rabbit hole
          goes—I don't wanna get tripped up
          with someone else's game on a
          higher level.

Manson leans his head back slightly, closing his eyes for a
moment as if trying to summon a memory from a past life.

                    CHARLES (CONT'D)
          Then this guy comes up with
          Dianetics. You know? Processing
          the mind... clearing the
          confusion, like scrubbing your soul
          with a steel brush. Be reborn
          within yourself. That was the
          hook. That's where Scientology
          really came from.

He nods slowly, like a preacher in his own chapel.

                    CHARLES (CONT'D)
          Then they started selling it, man.
          Like religion out the trunk of a
          Cadillac. Then it evolved into The
          Process... and then came the
          Church of the Final Judgment.
          That's where it all starts
          spiraling. End times, man. The
          last day.

He pauses again, listening to someone the camera can't see.

> CHARLES (CONT'D)
> I couldn't go myself—I had
> restrictions, y'know—but I sent
> people to England. Had 'em plant
> seeds. Stir things up, make an
> awakening. My man Bruce, yeah, he
> was one of 'em. He rode out that
> direction. But there were others
> on bikes, riding lines, doing
> shadow work. They didn't even know
> what they were doing—but the
> universe did.

Manson shifts in his seat. He raises his head, revealing a
faint mark on his forehead, almost like a faded scar or burn.
He taps it with one finger.

> CHARLES (CONT'D)
> You ever see them stones? That big
> pile over there? I think... if
> you go across those stones, you'll
> see this mark. Two... maybe three
> of those rocks got the same
> etching.

A twitch creeps across his lips—something like a smile,
something like dread.

> CHARLES (CONT'D)
> There's a lot goin' on with them
> stones. The occult's got layers,
> man. Stuff runnin' under the
> ground like roots—dark stuff.
> Nooses underground, twistin'
> through it all.

He stops. Looks up again. Eyes flicker toward the camera
and away.

> CHARLES (CONT'D)
> Would take too long to explain.
> But yeah... yeah, you're right.

Another pause. A hum of silence. Then he reacts to
something said off screen—almost scoffing.

> CHARLES (CONT'D)
> Whatever that means, man. God is
> the Devil, or the Devil is just a
> clever God, depending on which side
> you're standing on when the storm
> comes.

His voice turns jagged now, more urgent.

                         CHARLES (CONT'D)
              You wanna be all these individuals,
              believe all these truths—but then
              the wind shifts, and BAM—your truth
              don't mean shit. Now it hurts. So
              you twist. You change your mind.
              You got no choice, 'cause when it
              comes crashing down...

Manson leans forward, eyes wide with feverish energy.

                         CHARLES (CONT'D)
              You go down to the basement. And
              you're on the rack, man... tied
              up, screaming... and Manson?

He laughs darkly.

                         CHARLES (CONT'D)
                   (laughing through clenched
                    teeth)
              You're gonna do whatever the King
              tells you to do. It's that simple,
              man. That simple.

He sits back, breathing heavily. The sound of his chains
rattling fills the room. Behind him, the two prison guards
against the wall remain stone still, watching, unmoved.

The tape whines faintly. The time code jumps. Static creeps
across the screen.

END FLASHBACK.

EXT. 10050 CIELO DRIVE - LATE AFTERNOON - MARCH 23, 1969

The sun sinks low over the Benedict Canyon hills, casting
long, golden shadows across the winding private road that
leads to a secluded residence perched above Los Angeles.

This is 10050 Cielo Drive—a quiet, ivy-wrapped French country-
style estate hidden behind heavy foliage and a wooden gate.
The peaceful estate now belongs to Roman Polanski and his
wife, actress Sharon Tate, who is more than eight months
pregnant and scheduled to leave for Rome the following day.

From the outside, the scene is serene—a white convertible
parked in the circular drive, a sprinkler hissing quietly, a
light breeze rustling the trees.

But down the narrow road, a figure approaches on foot.
Small, wiry, and purposeful, Charles Manson walks with an odd
blend of intensity and calm.

He wears a dusty denim jacket, pants torn at the knees, and
boots caked with dust. His long, dark hair is tucked behind
his ears, his eyes shaded beneath his brow. He is not
smiling.

He is not expected.

EXT. FRONT PORCH - CIELO DRIVE - CONTINUOUS

SHAHROKH HATAMI, a polished, well-dressed Iranian
photographer in his late 30s, stands on the front porch of
the main house. A camera hangs from his neck, and a notebook
rests nearby on a patio table. He is preparing to photograph
Sharon Tate—a casual shoot before she departs for Europe.

Hatami spots the approaching man from the corner of his eye.
At first, he assumes it's a delivery or someone from the
groundskeeping crew—but the man's pace, his appearance, and
his presence quickly disabuse him of that assumption.

Hatami steps down cautiously from the porch and walks a few
feet forward, putting himself between the stranger and the
front door.

                    SHAHROKH HATAMI
                (excusing himself,
                 courteous but firm)
            Can I help you?

Manson slows. He stops several feet away, standing in the
shade of a tree.

                    CHARLES
            I'm looking for Terry Melcher.

Hatami blinks. The name doesn't register.

                    SHAHROKH HATAMI
            Melcher? I'm sorry... who?

                    CHARLES
            He used to live here.

Hatami gestures politely back toward the house.

                    SHAHROKH HATAMI
            This is the Polanski residence now.
            Roman Polanski, the film director.

Manson doesn't react. He stands silently, taking in the
house. There's something unnerving about the stillness in
him. His eyes are constantly moving, scanning the porch, the
windows, the roofline.

Behind Hatami, the front door opens slightly. SHARON TATE,
female white, 25, barefoot, dressed in a flowing cream
maternity dress, appears. Her blonde hair is pulled back
loosely, her hand resting on the edge of the doorway.

                    SHARON TATE
          Shahrokh? Who's that?

                    SHAHROKH HATAMI
               (quietly, over his
                shoulder)
          Just someone looking for the
          previous tenant.

She nods, eyes briefly locking with Manson's from across the
lawn. Her expression is neutral, curious. Manson says
nothing—just stares.

Hatami shifts again, uneasy. He gestures down a gravel path
that leads around the side of the main house toward the
guesthouse, which sits secluded at the back of the property.

                    SHAHROKH HATAMI (CONT'D)
          Maybe try the guesthouse. That's
          where the caretaker stays. Perhaps
          he knows more.

Manson glances down the path, then back at Hatami. His face
gives away nothing. Then, silently, he turns and walks
around the side of the house.

EXT. PATH TO GUESTHOUSE - MOMENTS LATER

Manson walks slowly toward the guesthouse, his boots
crunching the gravel. The property is quiet, except for the
sound of wind through trees and the faint clicking of
Hatami's camera shutter back at the main house.

He reaches the guesthouse and doesn't knock. He stands there
for a moment, looking at the door, then back toward the main
house. He lingers.

Then, after less than a minute, he turns around and walks
back toward the front.

EXT. FRONT OF THE HOUSE - CONTINUOUS

As he rounds the side, Hatami and Tate are still in view—both
watching him carefully.

Manson says nothing.

He doesn't wave, doesn't smile, doesn't acknowledge them. He passes the edge of the drive and continues walking down the hill the way he came, disappearing into the trees.

Hatami remains on the porch, a strange chill creeping down his spine. Tate watches the figure vanish, a hand now resting on her belly.

INT. CIELO DRIVE - LIVING ROOM - MOMENTS LATER

Hatami walks back inside and jots something in his notebook—just a passing note about the strange visitor. Sharon, already preparing for her Rome trip, brushes it off.

They don't speak of it again.

They couldn't have known...

That the man they saw that day would return.

EXT. 10050 CIELO DRIVE - EVENING

Night has settled over Benedict Canyon like a curtain of velvet. The sprawling Cielo Drive estate glows softly under porch lights and garden lamps, casting golden halos on the ivy-covered walls. The humming of insects mixes with the distant rustle of wind through sycamore trees. The air is warm but tense, as if holding its breath.

Charles Manson walks up the long gravel path for the second time that day, this time under cover of dusk. His silhouette blends into the shadows. His pace is deliberate, movements slow, calculating.

But he isn't heading toward the main house this time. Instead, he turns toward the guest house at the back of the property—a modest building tucked behind trees, lit only by a single porch bulb.

EXT. GUEST HOUSE - PORCH - CONTINUOUS

The screen door creaks slightly as Manson steps onto the porch, peering inside.

A moment later, the screen door opens just an inch. Standing behind it, RUDI ALTOBELLI, the property's owner, appears—still damp from the shower, a towel hanging loosely over his shoulder, shirt halfway buttoned.

Altobelli is in his early 40s, sharp-featured, with a tense air about him, like someone constantly managing people, money, and appearances.

His eyes narrow the moment he sees Manson.

              RUDI ALTOBELLI
        (flatly)
    Can I help you?

              CHARLES
        (quiet, smiling faintly)
    I'm looking for Terry Melcher.

A beat. Altobelli doesn't move from behind the screen.

              RUDI ALTOBELLI
    Melcher doesn't live here anymore.

Manson's eyes drift lazily over Altobelli, then toward the window behind him. There's something unreadable in his expression—more curiosity than threat, but not much less unsettling.

Altobelli stiffens.

              RUDI ALTOBELLI (CONT'D)
    He moved to Malibu.

Manson lingers, his gaze still locked on the interior of the guest house. His body language shifts—subtle, but enough to suggest that Melcher might not be the only reason he's here.

Altobelli senses it too.

              RUDI ALTOBELLI (CONT'D)
    I don't have his new address.

A lie.

Altobelli does have Melcher's address—but something instinctual holds him back from sharing it.

              CHARLES
    I was told to come around back.
    The folks in the main house—they
    sent me here.

Altobelli studies him for a moment.

              RUDI ALTOBELLI
    I'd appreciate it if you didn't
    disturb my tenants.

Another beat.

                    CHARLES
          You going somewhere?

                    RUDI ALTOBELLI
               (leaving no room for
                further conversation)
          I fly out tomorrow. I'll be
          overseas for a while.

                    CHARLES
          Maybe I'll come back when you
          return. I'd like to talk with you
          some more.

                    RUDI ALTOBELLI
          I'll be gone over a year.

Altobelli holds his gaze.

Manson doesn't argue, doesn't press. Just stands quietly.

Then, without another word, he turns and walks off the porch,
disappearing into the darkness between the trees, the faint
crunch of gravel fading behind him.

INT. LOS ANGELES INTERNATIONAL AIRPORT - TERMINAL - NEXT DAY
- MARCH 24, 1969

Sharon Tate, glowing with pregnancy, stylish in a travel
dress and sunglasses, waits beside Rudi Altobelli near their
boarding gate. The terminal bustles with movement, but a
lingering unease hangs over their quiet exchange.

As they walk toward the gate, Tate leans in close.

                    SHARON TATE
               (softly, almost casually)
          Was that... creepy-looking guy...
          did he come to see you last night?

Altobelli glances at her, surprised by her awareness.

                    RUDI ALTOBELLI
          Yes. He asked for Melcher.

Sharon doesn't reply immediately. She looks ahead through
the airport windows, into the California sun, brow furrowing
just slightly.

EXT. 10050 CIELO DRIVE - SAME TIME

The estate is quiet again. Sunlight gleams on the roof of the main house, on the path to the guest house. All seems normal.

But somewhere down the hill... Manson is watching.

EXT. SPAHN MOVIE RANCH - CHATSWORTH, CALIFORNIA - FALL 1968 TO SUMMER 1969

The sun burns low over the dusty canyons of Chatsworth, where the Spahn Movie Ranch, once a thriving set for Western films, now sits in decay. The rickety wooden buildings, saloon facades, and wagon wheels stand as crumbling relics of a bygone Hollywood. The animals are half-wild, the air always dry, and the silence unnatural.

But among the ruins, a new scene plays out—the rise of Charles Manson's "Family", a commune built not only on LSD and free love, but on apocalyptic prophecy and escalating paranoia.

Tex Watson, tall, easygoing, and fresh-faced, arrived at the ranch looking for belonging. Nine months later, he would become Manson's sword.

INT. SPAHN RANCH - MAIN CABIN - NIGHT

Inside the main cabin, Manson holds court. The walls flicker with firelight as the Family—mostly women, a few men—gather in a circle around him. Manson sits cross-legged, barefoot, strumming his guitar like a shaman with a thousand-yard stare.

Watson sits nearby, transfixed.

                    CHARLES
               (preaching)
          "Helter Skelter's comin', man. The
          black man's gonna rise. They'll
          kill all the pigs, all the
          whiteys—tear the system down. But
          when the smoke clears, they'll be
          lost... they'll look for a new
          leader. That's where we come in."

Watson nods slowly. In this haze of drugs, isolation, and constant repetition, logic begins to bend. He starts to believe what Manson says isn't madness—it's destiny.

Manson tells the group they are the chosen ones, destined to survive the coming race war by hiding in a bottomless pit in the desert. When the world tears itself apart, he—and by extension, they—will rule.

This is Helter Skelter.

EXT. LOS ANGELES STREET - NIGHT (JUNE 1969)

In the weeks before the violence, Manson's paranoia and desperation for resources to fund "Helter Skelter" intensify. He begins sending Family members on "creepy crawly missions" to steal, burglarize, and scavenge.

Tex Watson, now fully committed, steps forward to act on Manson's latest command:

"Find money. Now. Any way you can."

INT. APARTMENT - HOLLYWOOD - NIGHT

Watson meets with BERNARD "LOTSAPOPPA" CROWE, a large, imposing 22-year-old African American man known on the streets for his drug connections and fearsome reputation. Crowe is a friend of Watson's new lover, a streetwise woman who trusts Tex—but that trust is about to be shattered.

Tex, pretending to arrange a deal, manipulates Crowe into fronting money for a drug exchange that doesn't exist. Then Watson disappears—scamming Crowe without a second thought.

But Crowe isn't just any hustler.

He's furious. And he knows where Tex is hiding.

INT. SPAHN RANCH - DAY

A phone rings in one of the ranch's makeshift rooms. Manson answers.

>   CROWE
>   (from payphone)
>   Tell that boy Watson I'm coming.
>   And if I don't get my money
>   back—I'll kill every single one of
>   you.

Manson hangs up, his face tightening. He doesn't panic. He simmers.

                         CHARLES
              Blackie's trying to get at the
              chosen ones.

He grabs a .22-caliber revolver and heads into Hollywood.

INT. Manson's HOLLYWOOD APARTMENT - JULY 1, 1969 - NIGHT

The apartment is sparse. A tension hums through the air like
a wire pulled taut.

Crowe sits in a chair, arms crossed, posture defiant. His
bulk fills the room. He's unarmed, but Manson can feel the
threat oozing off him.

Manson enters, eyes cold and direct.

                      CHARLES (CONT'D)
              You threatened my Family.

                      BERNARD CROWE
              I want my money. Now.

Before another word is said, Manson pulls the gun and
fires—one round, point-blank, into Crowe's stomach. Crowe
slumps, moaning, blood spreading fast. Manson and another
Family member drag him into the hallway.

Manson flees, believing he's killed the man.

INT. SPAHN RANCH - MAIN CABIN - LATE AFTERNOON

A black-and-white television, its screen warped with static,
hums quietly in the corner of the room. The signal flickers
in and out. Family members lounge nearby, some folding
clothes, others sweeping the floor, half-listening.

Charles Manson sits on the edge of a worn sofa, elbows on
knees, face drawn tight with paranoia and calculation. He
stares blankly at the screen, not blinking, as the local news
plays.

A TV NEWS ANCHOR'S VOICE cuts through the static.

                      TV NEWS ANCHOR (V.O.)
              Authorities say the body of a
              man—believed to be a member of the
              Black Panthers—was discovered early
              this morning in South Los Angeles.
              The victim was found with a gunshot
              wound to the abdomen...

Manson leans forward, eyes narrowing.

>   TV NEWS ANCHOR (V.O.)
>   Police have not released the
>   identity of the victim at this
>   time. Sources suggest the shooting
>   may be gang-related...

Manson's jaw clenches. He clicks the television off
abruptly, the sudden silence louder than the broadcast.

>   CHARLES MANSON
>   (low, to himself)
>   That's him. Crowe. They dumped
>   him.

A few Family members look up. Manson slowly rises from the
couch and paces across the room.

>   CHARLES
>   They'll think we did it. They'll
>   want blood. The Panthers are
>   coming.

He turns, eyes burning.

>   CHARLES (CONT'D)
>   It's starting. Helter Skelter—it's
>   begun.

The others exchange worried glances. Manson storms out of
the cabin, issuing orders as he goes.

>   CHARLES MANSON (O.S.)
>   Get the rifles. Post lookouts.
>   Nobody sleeps tonight.

EXT. SPAHN RANCH - DAYS LATER

The ranch transforms overnight. Once a lazy commune, it
becomes a fortress. Armed night patrols begin. Knives,
guns, and axes are kept close. Every rustling leaf is
suspicious.

Manson brings in the Straight Satans Motorcycle Club, a group
of grimy, violent bikers, to act as security. Their presence
deepens the atmosphere of intimidation and chaos.

The Family members, especially the women, fall deeper into
obedience, terrified of both the outside world and
disappointing their leader.

INT. TEX WATSON'S CABIN - NIGHT

Watson stares at his reflection in a broken mirror. He's no
longer the kid from Texas who wanted love and freedom.

He's transformed—a soldier in a deluded war that hasn't yet
begun, but will soon.

Helter Skelter is no longer an idea.

It's about to become a reality.

EXT. SPAHN RANCH - DUSK - LATE JULY 1969

The sun hangs low over the arid, dust-covered hills
surrounding Spahn Ranch. The horses shuffle in their pens.
In the distance, the faint buzz of flies echoes off dry
wooden boards and broken wagon wheels. The mood at the ranch
is tense.

Manson paces, shirtless in the fading light, eyes darting
with growing paranoia. He's surrounded by Family
members—most of them barefoot, dazed, obedient—but the
pressure is boiling over. He sees shadows in every tree,
Black Panther retaliation in every gust of wind.

INT. SPAHN RANCH - MAIN CABIN - NIGHT

The room is dim. Candles burn low. The air is thick with
incense and tension.

Susan Atkins sits on the floor, cross-legged, drawing circles
in the dirt with her finger. Manson kneels beside her, his
tone soft, almost fatherly—but his eyes burn with something
far more sinister.

                    CHARLES
               (whispering)
          You said you wanted to be part of
          this... really be part of it.

Susan glances up. She nods.

                    CHARLES (CONT'D)
          There's something you can do.
          Something important.

She leans in. He strokes a strand of hair from her face.

                    CHARLES (CONT'D)
          There's a cat we used to crash
          with—Gary Hinman. He's got bread.
                    (MORE)

                    CHARLES (CONT'D)
          Lotta bread. Bobby says he came
          into money... inheritance or
          something. Gary's a nice guy.
          Music teacher. Thinks he's awake.

Susan frowns slightly.

                    CHARLES MANSON
          If you really love me... if you
          want this family to survive the
          storm coming... you'll go with
          Bobby. With Mary too. Ask Gary
          for what he owes. If he won't give
          it up...
               (A beat)
          ...you do what needs to be done.

Susan's expression hardens. She nods.

EXT. TOPANGA CANYON - GARY HINMAN'S HOUSE - DAY

Nestled in the hills of Topanga Canyon, Gary Hinman's modest
home is shaded by oaks and overgrown brush. A Volkswagen van
pulls up the dirt driveway. Inside: BOBBY BEAUSOLEIL, male
white, 22, Susan Atkins, and Mary Brunner.

Hinman's house is quiet. His motorcycle rests under a tarp,
musical instruments visible through the windows. A welcoming
man with a soft, bohemian air, Gary Hinman has opened his
door before to these wayward souls—offering shelter, food,
conversation.

Today is different.

INT. GARY HINMAN'S LIVING ROOM - CONTINUOUS

GARY HINMAN, male white, 34, gentle and introspective, opens
the door and greets them with a smile.

                    GARY HINMAN
          Susan. Mary. Bobby. What's going
          on?

                    BOBBY BEAUSOLEIL
          We need to talk.

Gary lets them in, sensing the weight behind Bobby's voice.

INT. GARY HINMAN'S HOUSE - LATER

They sit across from him, the mood now serious. Bobby leans forward.

                    BOBBY BEAUSOLEIL
          That mescaline you gave us... it
          was bad. The Straight Satans are
          pissed. They want their money
          back.

                    GARY HINMAN
               (uneasy)
          I didn't cut it. I got it from a
          solid connection. I tested it
          myself.

                    BOBBY BEAUSOLEIL
          They're saying they're gonna kill
          me if I don't make it right.

Hinman shakes his head.

                    GARY HINMAN
          It wasn't bad, Bobby. I don't have
          your money.

                    SUSAN ATKINS
               (quietly)
          Charlie says you just inherited
          like twenty grand.

Gary looks at her, confused and alarmed.

                    GARY HINMAN
          That's not true. I don't have that
          kind of money. I never said that.

Bobby stands up, pacing now.

                    BOBBY BEAUSOLEIL
          Don't lie to us, man. This is
          serious.

INT. HINMAN'S HOUSE - LATE NIGHT

Hours pass. Gary is now being held in his own home, watched carefully. Mary boils tea in the kitchen. Susan sits silently near the door.

Bobby paces again. Finally, he grabs the phone and calls Spahn Ranch.

INT. SPAHN RANCH - MAIN CABIN - NIGHT (INTERCUT)

Manson picks up, barefoot, coiled like a snake.

> BOBBY BEAUSOLEIL (V.O.)
> He's not giving it up, man. Says
> he doesn't have the money. Doesn't
> know what we're talking about.

A long pause.

> CHARLES
> Keep him there. Talk to him.
> Convince him. Don't leave 'til he
> gives it up. I'll come down.

CLICK.

INT. HINMAN'S HOUSE - CONTINUOUS

Bobby hangs up and turns back to Gary.

> BOBBY BEAUSOLEIL
> He's coming.

Gary's face tightens. He knows who "he" is.

> GARY HINMAN
> Bobby... don't do this.

> BOBBY BEAUSOLEIL
> You should've just given it to us.

EXT. TOPANGA CANYON - GARY HINMAN'S HOUSE - DAY - LATE JULY
1969

The winding roads of Topanga Canyon cut through dense
hillsides and quiet isolation. The air is still, the
rustling of leaves muffled beneath the hum of tension.

A beat-up Volkswagen van pulls up to the small, modest home
of Gary Hinman. Behind the wheel is Bruce Davis, Manson's
quiet, intense lieutenant. In the passenger seat: Charles
Manson, barefoot, eyes wild with fire and prophecy. Resting
across his lap is a samurai sword, its long blade glinting
ominously in the sun.

Manson opens the door, steps out slowly, and surveys the
house.

INT. HINMAN'S LIVING ROOM - MOMENTS LATER

Gary Hinman, already bruised and exhausted after being held
captive for nearly 24 hours, looks up from the couch where he
sits bound, trying to remain calm.

Mary Brunner and Susan Atkins linger in the background,
watching nervously. Bobby Beausoleil stands by the wall,
arms crossed, jaw clenched.

Manson enters the room like a shadow, Bruce Davis trailing
behind, expression unreadable.

                    CHARLES
               (quiet, cold)
          Still no money?

                    BOBBY BEAUSOLEIL
          He says he doesn't have any.

Manson walks directly to Gary and stands over him. Gary,
soft-spoken and spiritual, tries again.

                    GARY HINMAN
          Charlie... please. I've told you
          the truth. I don't have an
          inheritance. There's no money.

Without warning, Manson pulls the sword from his side and
slashes downward. The blade slices across Gary's left cheek,
the tip cleaving into his ear, nearly severing it.

Gary screams in agony, blood splashing onto his shirt and
down his neck. He writhes in place, but can't break free.

                    SUSAN ATKINS
               (sobbing)
          Charlie!

                    MARY BRUNNER
          Oh God... oh God...

Manson drops the sword, expression blank. He turns to
Beausoleil.

                    CHARLES
          You finish it. Get the money...
          or do what needs to be done.

He walks out, Bruce following behind without a word.

INT. HINMAN'S HOUSE - NIGHT

The hours drag into days.

Gary is tied to a chair, groaning, drifting in and out of
consciousness. His mutilated ear has been crudely stitched
back together with dental floss by Mary and Susan—a twisted
attempt at first aid. The wound is infected. He pleads for
medical help.

                    GARY HINMAN
               (weak, in pain)
          Please... just take me to the
          hospital... I swear... I have
          nothing.

But there is no sympathy left.

They feed him sporadically. They speak in whispers. Bobby
paces like a caged animal, torn between guilt and obedience.

At times, Gary chants softly, invoking Buddhist mantras,
trying to transcend the pain, the terror, the hopelessness.

INT. HINMAN'S HOUSE - THIRD NIGHT

It's over. Atkins, phone to her ear, somber expression,
listens. Manson's cold low tone voice comes over the
receiver.

                    CHARLES (V.O.)
          Kill him.

Gary is barely conscious, slumped on the floor, his breath
shallow. Bobby kneels beside him, holding a knife, hands
shaking.

Atkins walks up, a foreboding expression washes over her.

                    SUSAN ATKINS
          Charlie said it has to be now.

Bobby looks at Gary.

                    GARY HINMAN
               (whispers)
          Nam-myoho-renge-kyo... Nam-myoho-
          renge-kyo...

The chant is rhythmic, haunting. Beausoleil plunges the
knife into Gary's chest. Hinman gasps. Blood seeps out in
steady waves.

He doesn't die immediately. He gurgles, still muttering
prayers.

                    MARY BRUNNER
          Oh God, just end it.

Unable to bear it, they take turns holding a pillow over his
face, slowly pressing down until his movements cease.

INT. HINMAN'S LIVING ROOM - DAWN

The silence is deafening.

Bobby dips his hand into Gary's blood and walks to the wall.
With detached purpose, he writes:

"POLITICAL PIGGY"

Beneath it, he smears a bloody paw print—a crude attempt to
link the killing to the Black Panthers, part of Manson's
strategy to spark "Helter Skelter."

The scene now resembles a message from a phantom militia, not
a chaotic cult.

EXT. HINMAN'S DRIVEWAY - EARLY MORNING

Bobby Beausoleil exits the house, holding Gary's car keys.
He steps into Hinman's Fiat, wiping blood from his fingers
onto his pants.

The engine starts.

Bobby drives off in the murdered man's car, the words on the
wall bleeding into the shadows behind him.

INT. GARY HINMAN'S HOUSE - EARLY MORNING - CONTINUOUS

Mary Brunner and Susan Atkins move silently through the dimly
lit house. The air is heavy with blood and silence.

Mary kneels by the body, scrubbing the floor with a damp
cloth, her hands trembling. Blood seeps into the cracks of
the wooden boards.

Susan gathers discarded rags and soiled towels, stuffing them
into a paper bag. Her face is blank, her movements
mechanical. A window creaks as wind moves through the
canyon. Neither of them flinches. They work like
shadows—efficient, expressionless, and alone.

FLASHBACK:

INT. CALIFORNIA CORCORAN STATE PRISON - INTERVIEW ROOM - 1994

The screen flickers—grainy VHS footage, timestamped and slightly warped with static. The picture quality is poor. The color is washed out, as if the tape itself is degrading with time. The audio hums with low reverb, distorting the room's acoustics and making the voices feel hollow, distant.

Charles Manson, 60 years old, sits shackled in a heavy wooden chair, bolted to the floor. His hands are cuffed at the waist. His hair is long, greasy, parted unevenly, falling into his face. His mustache and goatee is patchy and gray. There is an odd gleam in his eyes, a gleeful tension that flutters in and out of his expressions like weather.

Two prison guards stand against the far wall—stone still, unspeaking.

Manson chuckles to himself, animated. His eyes dart to someone off-camera. He leans slightly forward, shifting in his restraints, reacting to an inaudible question or comment.

He grins, then suddenly turns inward—speaking as much to himself as to the unseen interviewer.

> CHARLES
> Little kids—yeah, little kids. I
> wanna hold your hand, you know?

He chuckles again. A sly, knowing grin spreads across his lips—then disappears.

> CHARLES (CONT'D)
> They still wanna hold my hand.
> Even now. Even after everything.
> They grow up, we grow up... but
> they're still just kids. All of
> 'em.

He shrugs.

> CHARLES (CONT'D)
> McCartney—or whatever his name
> is—don't know what he's doin'.
> He's makin' music with snakes, man.
> Got babies poppin' out all over the
> place. And he's just smilin',
> strummin', thinkin' he's some
> kinda... flower.

Manson's voice changes—harder now, accusatory.

> CHARLES (CONT'D)
> You don't lay with snakes, man.
> Sooner or later that thing's gonna
> bite you, chew you, swallow you
> whole.

He laughs, loud and sudden.

> CHARLES (CONT'D)
> And then you look down the
> street—HA-HA!—and you wonder why
> your kids are runnin' wild. Doin'
> things they never done before.
> Wearin' things you never wore.
> Dancin' in shadows, man.

He stops—squints, as if listening.

> CHARLES (CONT'D)
> Huh?

Manson leans slightly forward, frowning. His voice drops to
a quieter, more serious tone.

> CHARLES (CONT'D)
> Helter Skelter? That was their
> song, not mine. He wrote it.
> Didn't mean nothin' to me, not at
> first. But then the DA—he picks it
> up... makes it his. Makes it into
> a badge, a weapon, his trip.

Manson's expression darkens. His smile fades.

> CHARLES (CONT'D)
> They turned a song into a
> prophecy... and they put it in my
> mouth.

He sits back, muttering to himself, head tilting slightly
toward the ceiling, as if listening to voices only he can
hear.

The tape hisses.

A moment of static.

Then silence.

END FLASHBACK.

EXT. SPAHN RANCH - EVENING - AUGUST 8, 1969

The sun sets over the dusty, broken landscape of Spahn Ranch, casting deep amber light through the skeletal branches of eucalyptus trees. Shadows stretch across the rocky hills and crumbling facades of the old Western movie set. Horses stir in their corrals. Somewhere in the distance, coyotes begin to howl.

The air feels heavy. Something unseen and unspoken simmers in the atmosphere.

Near the front of the ranch, a dust-covered Ford Galaxie idles. The exhaust coughs intermittently, a faint mechanical rumble against the silence of the canyon.

A few yards away, Charles Manson stands on the gravel path, barefoot and shirtless, his eyes intense and unreadable in the fading light. Before him stand Susan Atkins, LINDA KASABIAN, female white, 20, and Patricia Krenwinkel—each woman seemingly dazed, yet focused, as if awaiting a ritual they don't fully understand.

Tex Watson, tall and lean with a drawl still clinging to his voice, stands slightly apart—silent, unreadable, ready.

Manson speaks in low, deliberate tones, his cadence almost hypnotic.

                    CHARLES
          You're going with Tex. Do
          everything he tells you. Don't ask
          questions. Don't hold back. Just
          do what needs to be done.

He paces slowly in front of them.

                    CHARLES (CONT'D)
          This is for Helter Skelter. It's
          time. No more waiting. You know
          what this is. We've talked about
          this. It's the beginning.

The women nod—nervous, detached, already under his spell.

Manson walks up to Linda Kasabian, the newest member, places his hand lightly on her shoulder.

                    CHARLES (CONT'D)
          You're the watcher. You see what
          needs to be seen. Don't let them
          get caught.

He turns to Watson.

                    CHARLES (CONT'D)
          Go to the house. Totally destroy
          everyone in it. And do it as
          gruesome as you can.

Manson's eyes flash with something primal—not rage, but
prophecy.

                    CHARLES MANSON
          Make it loud. Make it known.

Watson nods once.

The group climbs into the car.

INT. FORD GALAXIE - MOVING - NIGHT

The car drives along Mulholland Drive, winding through the
hills of Benedict Canyon. The city lights glow faintly
below, casting long silver reflections on the windows.

Inside the car: silence.

Tex Watson grips the wheel tightly, eyes focused. In the
passenger seat, Susan Atkins stares out the window, her
expression hardening with purpose.

Patricia Krenwinkel sits in the back beside Linda Kasabian,
her fingers nervously pulling at the hem of her dress. Linda
looks pale. Her breaths are shallow.

After several long minutes, Watson speaks.

                    TEX
          We're going to a house. Some rich
          people. We're gonna get money from
          them. Then we kill them.

No one reacts.

                    TEX (CONT'D)
          Charlie says we gotta start the war
          now. So we're gonna leave a
          sign... make it look like the
          Panthers. So they think it's them.

Another pause.

                    TEX (CONT'D)
          There's no mercy. No second
          thoughts. When we get there, you
          do what I say. Fast. Brutal.
          Don't hold back.

He looks at them each in the mirror.

                    TEX (CONT'D)
          This is for Helter Skelter.

The car continues silently through the hills. The road grows
narrower. A gate lies ahead.

EXT. CIELO DRIVE - GATE - NIGHT

The car pulls up to the gate at 10050 Cielo Drive.

Watson kills the lights and engine. He gets out quietly,
examining the gate. The stillness of the night hangs like a
curtain.

Behind this gate, the residents are unaware: Sharon Tate, Jay
Sebring, Wojciech Frykowski, and Abigail Folger.

Inside, they drink, laugh, and prepare for bed.

Outside, the agents of death approach—driven not by logic,
but by delusion, ideology, and blind obedience.

INT. CIELO DRIVE RESIDENCE - LIVING ROOM - NIGHT

Sharon Tate radiant even at eight and a half months pregnant,
sits barefoot on the couch in a flowing white maternity
dress. Her hand rests gently on her belly as she sips
chamomile tea, flipping through a fashion magazine. Her
movements are slow, graceful, tired.

She smiles gently as she watches her close friend and former
lover, JAY SEBRING, male white, 35, move around the room,
setting out records. A celebrated hairstylist to the stars,
Jay is sharply dressed even in casual wear—black slacks, a
crisp white shirt unbuttoned at the collar. He's attentive
to Sharon, checking on her comfort, occasionally brushing a
lock of hair from her face.

Their dynamic is tender, familiar—a deep, enduring friendship
forged through love and time.

INT. CIELO DRIVE - KITCHEN

WOJCIECH FRYKOWSKI, male white, 32, Polish, rugged and
slightly disheveled, stands at the counter, pouring glasses
of red wine. ABIGAIL FOLGER, female white, 25, elegant and
reserved, leans beside him. Dressed in a patterned summer
blouse and jeans, she hums quietly while cutting fruit into a
bowl.

Daughter of Peter Folger of the Folgers Coffee dynasty, Abby masks her upbringing with a bohemian edge, but her refinement is unmistakable. She hands a glass to Wojciech, and he clinks it gently.

                    WOJCIECH FRYKOWSKI
                (softly, in Polish)
          To peace and quiet.

They smile, unaware how fleeting that peace will be.

EXT. CIELO DRIVE - GROUNDS - SAME TIME

On the lower section of the property, near the garage and caretaker's cottage, WILLIAM GARRETSON, male white, 19, the estate's caretaker, listens to music in his room. The light is dim, the radio tuned to a late-night rock station. His mood is mellow, unaware of what's happening up the drive.

His friend, STEVEN PARENT, male white, 18, arrives shortly before 11 p.m. He's dropped by to visit Garretson and maybe sell him a clock radio. Parent is fresh-faced, polite, eager—dressed in a plaid shirt and jeans, he's just finished work and is heading home to El Monte.

The two chat briefly, Steven checking the time before deciding to head back down the driveway to his car.

INT. CIELO DRIVE - LIVING ROOM - LATER

The night unfolds with laughter and light conversation. Music hums from the stereo—The Mamas & the Papas, or maybe Simon & Garfunkel. The scent of wine, jasmine, and summer heat lingers in the air.

Sharon's friends do what friends do: they joke, they talk about movies, about Polanski in Europe working on his next film.

There's lightness in Sharon's voice, though a weariness behind her eyes.

                    SHARON TATE
                (with a wistful smile)
          I miss Roman, but he'll be back
          soon... before the baby.

Across the room, Jay pours another glass of wine, joking softly with Abigail. Frykowski stretches out on the floor beside the couch, eyes half-lidded.

                    JAY SEBRING
                 (casually)
            Quincy Jones was gonna stop by, but
            he flaked—lucky guy.

Unbeknownst to them, that flaked-out visit would save Quincy
Jones' life.

EXT. CIELO DRIVE - GATE - JUST AFTER MIDNIGHT - AUGUST 9,
1969

The canyon is still. Not silent—cicadas hum, a soft wind
rustles dry leaves—but eerily still, as if the land is
holding its breath.

A white utility pole rises beside the driveway's electronic
gate. At its base stands Charles "Tex" Watson, tall and
determined, gripping a pair of bolt cutters.

Behind him, Susan Atkins, Patricia Krenwinkel, and Linda
Kasabian wait in silence, cloaked in the shadows of scrub
brush and sycamores.

CLACK.

Watson climbs the pole with ease, trained and precise, and
cuts the phone line, severing the house from the outside
world in one quiet, deliberate motion.

He climbs down, his breath even.

They return to the dusty Ford Galaxie, parked discreetly at
the base of the hill, and back it further down the secluded
road, burying it in shadow. They step out, one by one, and
begin walking back up the long, dark incline toward the
house.

EXT. CIELO DRIVE - MAIN GATE - MINUTES LATER

They stop at the electronic gate, peering through its iron
bars. The estate sprawls beyond—lush trees, manicured
grounds, the main house faintly lit up like a sleepy palace.

Watson pauses, studying the panel beside the gate. He turns
to the others.

                    TEX
                 (whispering)
            Could be electrified. Or alarmed.
            We go around.

He leads them up the brushy embankment on the right side of
the gate, climbing through dirt, twigs, and dry undergrowth.
Their bare feet crunch softly over leaves and loose gravel.

One by one, they crest the hill and slip onto the property
grounds—ghosts crossing a boundary.

EXT. CIELO DRIVE - INSIDE THE GATE - MOMENTS LATER

They descend toward the house through a grove of pepper trees
and eucalyptus, hearts pounding.

Suddenly—

HEADLIGHTS.

An engine hums. A car begins rolling up the driveway from
the caretaker's guest house. The lights illuminate the
embankment—too fast, too close.

Watson reacts instantly.

                    TEX
          Get down.

Atkins, Krenwinkel, and Kasabian drop into the bushes,
pressing their bodies low, barely breathing.

Watson steps onto the driveway, his revolver drawn. The car
slows.

A white 1965 AMC Ambassador coupe pulls into view. Inside:
Steven Parent, glasses on, one hand resting on the wheel. He
squints, seeing a figure in the dark waving him down.

He slows to a stop.

EXT. CIELO DRIVE - DRIVER'S WINDOW - CONTINUOUS

Watson approaches the driver's side window. The revolver
glints in the moonlight. Steven Parent's expression shifts
from confusion to dread.

                    STEVEN PARENT
                (stammering)
          Please, don't—I won't say anything.
          I swear—please don't hurt me.

His voice cracks with panic.

Watson says nothing.

He raises the .22-caliber revolver, then suddenly lunges forward with a knife.

The blade slices into Steven's left palm as he instinctively tries to block the attack. The knife tears tendons, and his wristwatch falls away, flinging to the floorboard.

Parent screams, recoiling in pain—

BANG. BANG. BANG. BANG.

Four shots explode into the night.

Steven Parent is struck in the chest and abdomen, slumping against the driver's seat. Blood spatters the dashboard. The coupe falls silent, headlights still on, engine idling gently as the teenager lies motionless in the front seat.

Watson breathes heavily, staring through the windshield for a moment, then turns back to the bushes.

                    TEX
          Come on. Help me move the car.

EXT. CIELO DRIVE - DRIVEWAY - MOMENTS LATER

The women emerge cautiously from the brush, visibly shaken. Together, they push the blood-smeared coupe a short way up the driveway—far enough to keep it hidden in shadow, tucked against the embankment.

None of them speak.

The night air feels tighter now. Something has shifted.

The first blood has been spilled.

And they are only getting started.

EXT. 10050 CIELO DRIVE - SIDE OF HOUSE - AFTER MIDNIGHT - AUGUST 9, 1969

The grounds of the estate are quiet, still as a painting. The wind has died. Even the crickets seem to have silenced themselves.

Tex Watson crouches in the shadows near a side window. In his hand: a long-bladed buck knife and a .22 caliber revolver tucked into his waistband. His face is grim, jaw clenched in ritualistic resolve.

He examines the screened window—one of the few that isn't alarmed. From within, a faint interior light spills onto the grass. Shadows flicker beyond the curtain—movement. Breathing. Sleep.

Watson reaches into his pocket and pulls out a hunting knife, then slices the mesh screen cleanly, silently, his hand practiced. The blade moves like a scalpel.

He looks back at the women: Susan Atkins, Patricia Krenwinkel, and Linda Kasabian, all crouched behind the thick foliage near the driveway.

                    TEX
                (whispers)
        Kasabian—go watch the gate.

Kasabian nods silently, nervous, lips trembling. She glances toward the house, then turns and walks briskly back down the gravel driveway, retracing her steps to where Steven Parent's corpse still lies in the front seat of his car.

She doesn't look at the body. She can't.

She positions herself behind a tree with a clear view of the front gate—the lookout.

EXT. WINDOW - CONTINUOUS

Watson carefully lifts the screen free, leans in, and hoists himself into the window frame, lowering one leg into the darkened room.

Inside, the air is thick and still. He moves like a shadow—quiet, predatory.

INT. CIELO DRIVE - LIVING ROOM - MOMENTS LATER

The house is beautiful. Expensive. Tasteful. A white rug sprawls across the hardwood floor. On the couch lies Wojciech Frykowski, asleep in his clothes, his arm draped over the cushion.

Watson moves silently across the room and disappears toward the front hallway.

Seconds later, the front door clicks open.

Susan Atkins and Patricia Krenwinkel slip inside.

The door closes softly behind them. The spell of silence remains.

Watson motions to Atkins—points to the couch.

She nods.

He steps forward toward Frykowski and—without warning—kicks him in the head.

THUD.

Frykowski jolts awake, groaning in confusion and pain, lurching up from the cushions. Dazed, he stares at the three intruders looming over him.

> WOJCIECH FRYKOWSKI
> (disoriented)
> What... who are you? What the
> hell are you doing in my house?

He starts to rise, but Watson steps forward, leveling the revolver right at his face.

> TEX
> (quietly, with chilling
> calm)
> I'm the devil... and I'm here to
> do the devil's business.

Frykowski freezes.

The room suddenly feels like it's collapsing inward—everything warm and safe replaced by a cold gravity of imminent death.

Atkins moves toward the hallway, knife in hand.

Krenwinkel follows behind her, eyes scanning for the others inside.

The household of dreams has become a house of terror.

INT. CIELO DRIVE - LIVING ROOM - MINUTES AFTER ENTRY - AUGUST 9, 1969

Wojciech Frykowski sits upright, blood already streaking from the gash on his head from Watson's boot. His breathing is erratic, panic building. The warm comfort of sleep is long gone—replaced by confusion and the cold grip of fear.

Tex Watson, revolver steady in his hand, keeps Frykowski at bay as Susan Atkins and Patricia Krenwinkel fan out through the house.

INT. CIELO DRIVE - BEDROOMS - CONTINUOUS

Atkins creaks open the door to the master bedroom—and there lies Sharon Tate, sitting up in bed, eyes wide, already disturbed by the noise. In the dim lamp light, her eight-and-a-half-month pregnant belly is unmistakable.

Atkins levels her knife.

                    SUSAN ATKINS
          Get up. Now. You're coming with
          me.

Tate hesitates, frozen by disbelief. But when Atkins steps forward and grabs her arm, she obeys.

Krenwinkel moves toward another door—she opens it and finds Abigail Folger, seated in bed reading. Abigail looks up, startled.

                    PATRICIA KRENWINKEL
          Out. Now. Don't speak.

Abigail rises slowly. Her face pales.

At the far end of the hallway, Jay Sebring, also alerted by the noise, steps into the corridor in a robe. He freezes as he sees the two armed women herding the others.

                    JAY SEBRING
          What the hell is going on?

Watson enters the hallway behind him, gun raised.

                    TEX
          Back to the living room. Everyone.

INT. CIELO DRIVE - LIVING ROOM - MOMENTS LATER

Now all four victims are gathered in the center of the living room. Their faces reflect a mix of terror, disbelief, and anger.

Sharon Tate, trembling, holds her arms protectively around her stomach. Jay Sebring instinctively positions himself between her and the attackers.

Watson removes a long nylon rope from his pocket. He tosses it over one of the exposed wooden ceiling beams, creating a makeshift noose.

                    TEX
                 (quietly)
          On the floor. Tie them.

He orders Atkins and Krenwinkel to begin binding their
victims.

Watson wraps one end of the rope around Tate's neck, the
other end around Sebring's, securing the two together and
then pulling the rope taut so that any sudden movement from
either would tighten the noose around both.

Sebring grits his teeth.

                 JAY SEBRING
          She's pregnant, for God's sake.
          Take me instead—don't hurt her.

Watson steps forward—without hesitation—and shoots Sebring in
the chest.

BANG.

Sharon screams. Blood blooms across Sebring's shirt as he
collapses backward, gasping. He convulses but remains alive.

Sharon cries out in shock and panic, now tethered to his
fallen body by the rope at her neck.

Krenwinkel grabs Abigail by the arm and begins pulling her
toward the hallway.

                 PATRICIA KRENWINKEL
          Get your purse. We want money.

They return to the bedroom. Abigail, still shaking, reaches
into her dresser and retrieves her wallet. She pulls out $70
in cash and hands it over without resistance.

                 ABIGAIL FOLGER
          Take it. Please, just take it.

INT. CIELO DRIVE - LIVING ROOM - MOMENTS LATER

Watson now turns back to Sebring, who is gasping on the
floor, his face twisted in agony.

Without a word, Watson plunges his knife into Sebring's body.

Once. Twice. Again. Seven times total.

Sebring's blood pools around him as his body goes limp.

Suddenly, a sharp yell—Frykowski has broken free.

INT. LIVING ROOM TO FRONT PORCH - CONTINUOUS

Frykowski, his hands loosely bound with a towel, thrashes and shoves Atkins aside. Her knife catches his leg, leaving a slash across his thigh. He yells in pain but barrels forward, desperate.

He stumbles through the living room, past the bodies, and bursts through the front door onto the porch.

He makes it ten feet.

Then—Watson is behind him.

Watson raises the gun and swings it like a club, striking Frykowski in the head.

CRACK.

Frykowski drops to his knees, blood pouring from his scalp.

Watson mounts him, stabbing again and again. Over the chest. The back. The shoulders.

Then—two final gunshots.

BANG. BANG.

Frykowski's body slumps at the edge of the porch, his life extinguished. Blood soaks the brick steps.

Inside, chaos reigns.

Tate is sobbing, staring at Sebring's corpse. Folger trembles, eyes darting between exits. The rope now connects the living to the dead.

The massacre is far from over.

EXT. CIELO DRIVE - DRIVEWAY - 12:45 A.M. - AUGUST 9, 1969

Linda Kasabian stands by Steven Parent's parked car, her arms wrapped around herself, barely breathing. Her position gives her a view of the front gate, but her mind is elsewhere—up the hill, where the house looms in shadow and sound.

Then it happens.

Screams.

Not a single shriek—but layers of terror, a symphony of
horror: voices raised in agony, panic, violence.

Kasabian flinches.

The noise is unmistakable now—gunshots, a woman's sobs, and
something else: shouting, thrashing, something heavy crashing
against walls or floors.

> LINDA KASABIAN
> (softly, to herself)
> Oh my God...

Her legs move without thought. She starts up the
hill—compelled by dread. As she reaches the front yard, she
sees Susan Atkins emerge from the doorway, blood spattered
across her clothing, face wild.

> LINDA KASABIAN (CONT'D)
> (breathless)
> Someone's coming... from down the
> road. You should stop—someone's
> coming.

It's a lie. A desperate attempt to interrupt the massacre.

Atkins doesn't respond—her eyes are locked in a manic daze.

INT. CIELO DRIVE - BEDROOM TO POOL AREA - MOMENTS LATER

Abigail Folger had seen her chance.

With Watson and Atkins distracted by Frykowski and Tate,
Folger breaks free from Krenwinkel's grip, darting toward the
bedroom door. She flings it open and bolts into the cool
night air, heading for the pool.

Her bare feet slap against the stone patio as she sprints.

Her white nightgown, once elegant, now stained red, flutters
behind her like a banner of desperation.

EXT. FRONT LAWN - SECONDS LATER

Patricia Krenwinkel tears out of the house in pursuit. Her
knife is clenched tightly in her hand, her breath ragged.
She spots Abigail veering off course toward the front lawn,
trying to circle around the house and find a way out.

Krenwinkel lunges.

She catches Abigail by the shoulder and tackles her to the grass, dragging her down hard.

                    ABIGAIL FOLGER
                  (screaming)
              No—please—please!

Abigail kicks and fights, but Krenwinkel is on top of her, slashing wildly.

Blood arcs into the grass.

Abigail manages to pull away, stumbling forward—only to have Watson catch up from behind, knife in hand.

Together, they descend.

Twenty-eight stab wounds.

Abigail's screams fade to gasps... then silence.

Her body lies motionless beneath the stars, white nightgown soaked crimson, blending with the blood-soaked grass.

EXT. FRONT LAWN - NEARBY - SAME TIME

Wojciech Frykowski, still alive, crawls across the lawn, leaving a wide smear of blood beneath him. His body is torn, broken—his will to live the only thing left carrying him forward.

But Watson sees him.

He moves quickly, stepping over Abigail's body, rage now mechanical, detached.

He catches up to Frykowski, grabs his shoulder, and slams the butt of his gun into the back of his skull.

CRACK.

Then again. And again.

Thirteen blows. One side of the gun grip snaps off, later found in the bushes. The barrel is bent inward from the force.

Still, Watson isn't done.

He stabs Frykowski repeatedly—fifty-one times in total. Chest, back, shoulders, arms. The violence is relentless, as if trying to erase him from existence.

Frykowski finally stops moving.

The lawn is a battlefield now—two bodies lie twisted in separate pools of blood. The night is utterly silent, save for the distant hum of Los Angeles and the slow breathing of the murderers.

EXT. CIELO DRIVE - YARD - CONTINUOUS

Kasabian stands paralyzed.

She can't stop it.

She can only watch as death spreads across the property like a shadow, inching toward the final victim.

INT. CIELO DRIVE - LIVING ROOM - MOMENTS LATER - AUGUST 9, 1969 - AFTER 1:00 A.M.

The once-beautiful home is now a chamber of horror.

The white carpet is soaked in blood—thick, smeared footprints track from room to room. Furniture is overturned. Glass shattered. The walls seem to echo with the aftermath of screams that have stopped too suddenly.

Sharon Tate, stands bound, her neck still tethered by the nylon rope that once connected her to Jay Sebring's corpse. Her arms tremble violently, blood running down her nightgown from shallow slashes already inflicted.

Her breath hitches. Her voice shakes.

                    SHARON TATE
          Please... please don't kill me.
          You can take me with you. Hold me
          hostage. Just let me have my baby.

Her hands cradle her swollen belly, fingers interlaced in desperate protection. She steps back from Susan Atkins and Tex Watson, who now face her—expressionless, blood-spattered, hollowed out.

Watson tightens his grip on the knife.

Atkins watches Sharon with a strange calm—a mix of awe, disgust, and detachment.

                    SHARON TATE (CONT'D)
                 (tears streaming)
          You can kill me later, I swear…
          just let him be born.

Watson says nothing.

Then he lunges.

The first stab lands in Sharon's chest. A scream erupts—but only one.

She doesn't run.

She doubles over slightly, tears still falling as blood blooms through the thin fabric of her nightgown.

Watson stabs again. And again.

Atkins joins in.

Her blade plunges fast and erratic. One arm grips Sharon's shoulder; the other works the knife with brutal efficiency.

Sharon cries out once more, but her voice gives way to gurgling breath. Her knees collapse beneath her.

Sixteen wounds in total—from both hands, from both killers.

When she finally hits the ground, her body lands next to Jay's, the rope coiling like a serpent between them. Her hand rests gently on her stomach, frozen there, her final act of defiance—to protect the unborn life inside her.

But it's too late.

INT. CIELO DRIVE - FOYER - MINUTES LATER

A hush falls over the house. Only the sound of footsteps sloshing through blood, and the occasional nervous breath.

Susan Atkins stands in the entrance hall, staring at the front door—her knife still in her hand. Her face is smeared, her eyes glassy.

She looks back toward the carnage, then down at her hand—coated in blood.

A thought sparks. A ritual. A message.

> SUSAN ATKINS
> (softly)
> Leave a sign. Something witchy...

She raises her hand and presses her fingers to the door—writing with Tate's blood.

P I G

The letters smear slightly, thick and deep red, dripping down the painted wood.

It mirrors what they'd written at Gary Hinman's home, the words scrawled in blood there by Bobby Beausoleil, who now sits in jail. This—this is supposed to send a signal, a copycat killing to confuse police and, hopefully, get Bobby out.

To the killers, it is not just slaughter. It is strategy cloaked in madness.

EXT. CIELO DRIVE - NIGHT - CONTINUOUS

Outside, Linda Kasabian stands near the gate, pale, unmoving. The silence is unbearable.

She sees the others emerge from the house—Watson, Atkins, Krenwinkel—blood on their hands, clothes, arms.

No words are exchanged.

Just nods.

They leave like shadows, fading into the hills, swallowed by the void they created.

EXT. 10050 CIELO DRIVE - MORNING - AUGUST 9, 1969

INSERT CARD: 7:45 A.M.

The sun rises slowly over Benedict Canyon, casting golden rays through the treetops. The morning mist clings to the edges of the driveway, softening the world. The house at 10050 Cielo Drive sits still—too still—as if frozen in time.

A car pulls up to the front gate, and WINIFRED CHAPMAN, a well-dressed Black woman in her 50s, steps out. She holds her purse close, clutching keys and a folded newspaper.

Dressed modestly for work, Winifred's eyes scan the quiet property. She's been the housekeeper for Roman Polanski and Sharon Tate for several months now. The job is reliable. The people kind. This morning was supposed to be like any other.

She presses the gate buzzer. Nothing.

She tries again. No response.

Her brow furrows.

EXT. CIELO DRIVE - FRONT GATE - MOMENTS LATER

Winifred sighs and pulls out the spare key Polanski left for
her. She unlocks the pedestrian gate and begins walking up
the long gravel driveway. The air is still. Her shoes
crunch the stones beneath her feet.

Halfway up the drive, something catches her eye—just ahead,
parked near the edge of the embankment.

A white AMC Ambassador.

Its driver's side window is shattered. The interior is
splashed with blood. A young man slumps inside—lifeless,
head tilted back, eyes open.

Winifred stops in her tracks.

She stares. Frozen.

Then her hand flies to her mouth.

                    WINIFRED CHAPMAN
          Oh my God...

She backs away. Instinctively. But she has to know what's
happened. She hurries past the car, toward the house.

EXT. CIELO DRIVE - ENTRYWAY - MOMENTS LATER

The front door is ajar.

Not just unlocked—slightly open.

She hesitates. Every part of her body says go back, but she
reaches out and pushes the door slowly.

It creaks open.

The first thing she sees is the word "PIG" scrawled in blood
across the lower panel of the door.

The newspaper drops from her hands.

INT. CIELO DRIVE - FOYER / LIVING ROOM - CONTINUOUS

She steps inside and gasps.

The house is in ruins—overturned furniture, broken glass,
deep smears of blood across the white carpet.

And then—the bodies.

She sees Jay Sebring, lying motionless in a pool of dried blood near the couch.

A few feet away, Sharon Tate, still in her white nightgown, tethered by a rope to Sebring's neck. Her eyes are half open. Her face is still. Her body, eight months pregnant, has been stabbed multiple times.

Winifred screams.

>   WINIFRED CHAPMAN
>   (sobbing)
>   No! No! Oh my God! Help!
>   Somebody help!

She stumbles backward, barely able to stand.

She rushes out of the house, hands trembling, breath coming in ragged gasps.

EXT. NEIGHBORING HOUSE - MINUTES LATER

Winifred pounds on the door of a nearby property—the home of a private caretaker. The door opens, and she collapses in the doorway, sobbing.

>   WINIFRED CHAPMAN
>   They're dead! They're all dead!

The caretaker helps her inside. The police are called.

The nightmare at Cielo Drive is now in motion—shocking the world by afternoon.

EXT. SPAHN RANCH - NIGHT - AUGUST 9, 1969

The moon hangs low in the sky over the dusty grounds of Spahn Ranch, casting long shadows across the worn-out barns and abandoned props of the old Western movie set.

Inside the ranch house, Charles Manson paces slowly, silent and brooding. The murders at Cielo Drive are only hours old, but something in him still festers—a hunger, a dissatisfaction, a need for something grander.

Nearby, Tex Watson, Susan Atkins, Patricia Krenwinkel, and Linda Kasabian sit close, drained but alert. Their clothes still bear the stains of the previous night's slaughter. They await Manson's next command with the reverence of cult-like loyalty—and the fear of failing him again.

Manson finally stops pacing.

                    CHARLES
          Last night... it was messy.
          Sloppy. No soul in it.

He turns to face them, voice low, like a sermon.

                    CHARLES (CONT'D)
          They didn't get the message. We
          have to make it clearer. Bigger.
          Make it echo.

He points at Kasabian.

                    CHARLES (CONT'D)
          Get the station wagon.

Kasabian nods.

EXT. LOS ANGELES STREETS - LATER THAT NIGHT - MOVING

The Family station wagon winds through the darkened streets
of Los Angeles, its headlights cutting through the quiet
suburban night. Manson rides in the front seat, Kasabian
driving. Behind them sit Watson, Atkins, Krenwinkel, and now
joined by Leslie Van Houten and STEVE "CLEM" GROGAN, male
white, 18.

The air inside the station wagon is heavy. No one speaks.
Even those high on Manson's ideology sense something darker
tonight—a shifting from chaos into mission.

Manson leans forward, peering out into the cityscape as they
pass rows of sleeping houses.

                    CHARLES
          Turn here. We're going to Waverly.

Kasabian obeys without question.

EXT. WAVERLY DRIVE - LOS FELIZ - EARLY A.M. HOURS - AUGUST
10, 1969

The station wagon turns onto Waverly Drive, a hilly
residential street nestled in the quiet neighborhood of Los
Feliz. Trees line the street, casting shadows on sidewalks
and rooftops.

Manson scans the houses until his eyes settle on one: 3301
Waverly Drive.

It's a single-story, Spanish-style home with a neatly trimmed
lawn and iron-railed front porch. The lights inside are low.
The house looks calm. Peaceful.

Manson leans back.

> CHARLES
> This one.

There's a pause in the station wagon.

> LINDA KASABIAN
> (softly)
> We've been here before, haven't we?

> CHARLES
> Next door. Party. Last year.

Indeed, Manson and several Family members had once attended a
gathering at the neighboring house. He remembers it
clearly—the music, the strangers, the feeling of not
belonging. But this house—Leno and Rosemary LaBianca's
home—was quiet. Tidy. A symbol of middle-class comfort.

Manson stares at the house, as if he can see inside.

> CHARLES (CONT'D)
> They live well. They need to feel
> it.

He opens the station wagon door.

> CHARLES (CONT'D)
> Let's wake them up.

He steps into the night, and the rest of the Family watches
as he moves through the darkness toward the house—not to
kill, not yet—but to scout, to control the energy, to pave
the way for what's coming.

INT. 3301 WAVERLY DRIVE - BEDROOM - SAME TIME

Inside, LENO LaBIANCA, male white, 44, a stocky man with
slicked-back hair, snores lightly in his bed. His wife,
ROSEMARY, female white, 43, elegant and thoughtful, lies
beside him, turned away, resting peacefully.

Neither of them has any idea that death is now watching from
the shadows outside their home.

EXT. 3301 WAVERLY DRIVE - LOS FELIZ - EARLY A.M. - AUGUST 10,
1969

The street is dead silent, the glow of the occasional porch
light reflecting off the leaves. The station wagon sits
idling a block away. Inside, Manson leans forward.

                    CHARLES
          Wait here.

Without another word, Manson slips out of the vehicle,
gliding up the sidewalk toward the LaBianca home like a
shadow. His eyes flick over the familiar property—a house of
comfort, now targeted for chaos.

He walks up the long driveway, keeping low. At the back of
the house, he tries the rear door.

Unlocked.

He disappears inside.

INT. LA BIANCA HOUSE - MOMENTS LATER

Leno LaBianca, lies asleep on the living room couch, snoring
softly, the remnants of a Sunday newspaper folded across his
chest. On the coffee table sits a half-finished glass of
milk.

Manson tiptoes across the carpeted floor. His hand tightens
around the handle of the revolver he's brought. Quietly, he
kneels beside the couch and places the cold steel barrel
against Leno's throat.

                    LENO LABIANCA
                 (startled awake)
          Wha—what is this?

                    CHARLES
          Don't move. You're just being
          robbed.

EXT. BACKYARD - A MINUTE LATER

Manson opens the back door and gestures to Tex Watson,
waiting in the shadows.

                    CHARLES
          Come on.

Watson enters with steady resolve. As they creep past the
kitchen, Manson points silently to the living room window,
where Leno sits now—awake, terrified, but not resisting.

> CHARLES (CONT'D)
> (managing calm)
> Help me tie him.

INT. LIVING ROOM - CONTINUOUS

Watson steps up. They use a leather thong—part of Leno's own
belt—to bind his wrists behind his back. Manson assures him
again:

> CHARLES
> You're not gonna be hurt. We just
> want the money.

But that's a lie.

> CHARLES (CONT'D)
> (to Watson)
> Stay with him.

Manson then walks down the hallway.

INT. MASTER BEDROOM - MOMENTS LATER

Rosemary LaBianca, is asleep in bed, unaware of the presence
of death in her home.

Manson flips on the light.

Rosemary bolts upright, gasping.

> CHARLES
> Come with me. Don't scream.

She stumbles out of bed in her nightgown, bewildered and
terrified. Manson leads her to the living room, where Leno's
eyes widen upon seeing his wife escorted at gunpoint.

Manson tells her the same lie:

> CHARLES (CONT'D)
> (to Rosemary)
> It's just a robbery.

Then he orders Watson to put pillowcases over their heads,
and to tie them in place with lamp cords. The room
darkens—figuratively—as the two LaBiancas, blinded and bound,
sit silently on the couch, breathing hard.

Manson steps back, satisfied.

He turns and walks to the door.

                    CHARLES (CONT'D)
          I'm going.

EXT. WAVERLY DRIVE - OUTSIDE THE HOUSE - MINUTES LATER

Manson returns to the station wagon and speaks quietly to
Krenwinkel and Van Houten.

                    CHARLES
          Go help Tex. You know what to do.

Without question, they exit the station wagon and move toward
the house.

Manson climbs back in and waits in the darkness.

INT. LA BIANCA HOUSE - LIVING ROOM - MOMENTS LATER

Inside, Watson, now alone with the couple, looks over the
poorly suited weapons—a bayonet, kitchen knives. He had
complained earlier that they weren't good enough for this
kind of work.

But now, he improvises.

He instructs the women to take Rosemary back to the bedroom,
leaving Leno seated on the couch, blindfolded, breathing
through shallow panic.

INT. BEDROOM - CONTINUOUS

Krenwinkel and Van Houten lead Rosemary in, hands bound, head
covered. She resists slightly, but she's confused,
disoriented. A lamp cord remains tied around her neck, the
heavy bedside lamp swinging from it as she walks.

INT. LIVING ROOM - CONTINUOUS

Watson steps forward, bayonet in hand.

Without a word, he plunges it into Leno's throat.

Leno grunts in pain and kicks forward, still blinded. Watson
stabs again—repeatedly—until the couch is soaked in blood.

INT. BEDROOM - SAME TIME

A sudden commotion—Rosemary screams and thrashes. The lamp
tied around her neck becomes a weapon, swinging violently as
she fights off Krenwinkel and Van Houten.

Watson storms into the room and plunges the bayonet into
Rosemary.

Her scream chokes in her throat.

He stabs her again.

And again.

Her knees collapse under her. Her body twitches with the
last nerve reflexes of life.

INT. LIVING ROOM - MINUTES LATER

Watson returns to Leno, who now lies half-slumped, still
gasping faintly. He resumes his attack.

Twelve stab wounds.

Each one deeper than the last.

Then Watson pulls out the blade and carves a word into Leno's
stomach—

W-A-R

The letters are crooked, jagged, oozing red across his belly.

INT. BEDROOM - MOMENTS LATER

Van Houten steps forward, face blank. Her knife rises.

She stabs Rosemary's back over and over—sixteen times—into
her lower back and exposed buttocks.

By now, Rosemary no longer moves.

Krenwinkel continues stabbing with a knife taken from the
kitchen.

There is no sound now except for the squelch of metal against
flesh.

INT. BATHROOM - MOMENTS LATER

Watson stands in the shower, rinsing the blood from his arms
and face. The water runs red down the drain.

INT. KITCHEN / LIVING ROOM - LATER

Krenwinkel steps to the walls.

She dips a rag into Leno's blood and begins writing:

On one wall:

"Rise"

On another:

"Death to Pigs"

On the refrigerator door:

"Helter Skelter"

All in thick, blood-red strokes.

She walks back to the body of Leno and grabs an ivory-
handled, two-pronged carving fork from the kitchen drawer.

With ritualistic calm, she stabs it into his stomach, letting
the handle jut out like a grotesque ornament.

Then, she drives a steak knife into his throat and leaves it
embedded there.

EXT. WAVERLY DRIVE - MINUTES LATER

The three killers return to the station wagon.

They do not speak.

They disappear into the night—leaving death, chaos, and
madness behind.

EXT. VENICE, CALIFORNIA - PARKING LOT NEAR PACIFIC AVENUE -
PRE-DAWN HOURS - AUGUST 10, 1969

The air is cool and salty near the coast as Manson's car
pulls up quietly near a run-down apartment complex in Venice.
The street is dark, only dimly illuminated by a flickering
streetlamp and the neon of a closed liquor store across the
road.

Inside the car are Susan Atkins, Linda Kasabian, and Steve "Clem" Grogan—each in various states of fatigue and nerves after hours of being shuttled around by Manson, who has now grown impatient and erratic.

> CHARLES
> (pointing toward the
> building)
> That's it. That's where he lives.
> Saladin. The guy's a pig—an actor.
> Thinks he's clever. You go up and
> take care of it.

Atkins and Grogan nod, sluggish but willing. Kasabian, behind the wheel earlier that night, remains tight-lipped.

Manson stares at her a little longer—suspicious, perhaps sensing her hesitancy—but says nothing.

He throws the car into reverse and begins backing out.

> CHARLES (CONT'D)
> I'll see you at the ranch. Find
> your way back.

And just like that, he's gone, the taillights disappearing into the early morning gloom.

EXT. STAIRWELL - SALADIN NADER'S APARTMENT COMPLEX - MOMENTS LATER

The trio walks up the narrow concrete stairwell toward the second floor. The building is quiet, the halls echoing their footsteps. A slight breeze rolls through the open hallway, carrying the sharp tang of the ocean.

Susan Atkins clutches a kitchen knife, her hands still red under the nails from the LaBianca massacre earlier that night. Her expression is cold, mechanical. Grogan, high and barely focused, trails behind her.

Linda Kasabian walks in front, silent.

She knows the apartment number. She's been here before.

Saladin Nader is someone she met during a previous encounter, someone she had spoken to. She knows exactly where he lives.

But as they reach the correct door, Kasabian suddenly slows.

She looks at the door. She knows what will happen if they go through it.

She turns—and walks two doors further down the hall.

Without a word, she raises her fist and bangs loudly on the wrong door.

KNOCK. KNOCK. KNOCK.

A light flicks on inside.

There's movement. A voice from within.

> STRANGER (O.S.)
> Who's there? It's 4 A.M., what the
> hell?

Kasabian's heart races. She steps back.

> LINDA KASABIAN
> (to Atkins, whispering)
> Wrong door. Let's go. We have to
> go.

Confused and irritated, Atkins and Grogan follow her quickly down the stairs. They don't press the issue. Their adrenaline is low. Their judgment foggy.

But before they exit—

Susan Atkins stops.

She looks back up the stairwell with disdain.

> SUSAN ATKINS
> (grimacing)
> Pigs everywhere.

Then, in an act of pure contempt, she squats down at the top of the stairwell and defecates on the concrete landing—a final mark of defilement, aimed at no one in particular, but born of rage and madness.

Kasabian recoils, but doesn't speak.

Grogan laughs, barely understanding.

Then they slip into the darkness, fading into the empty Venice streets, with only the sound of ocean waves in the distance.

EXT. PACIFIC AVENUE - MINUTES LATER

The three of them walk in silence.

No murder. No message. No blood.

And yet the night feels poisoned just the same.

As they disappear into the city, Kasabian keeps her eyes ahead, quietly knowing she saved a life, even as the weight of what was done hours earlier hangs heavy around her neck.

FLASHBACK:

INT. CALIFORNIA CORCORAN STATE PRISON - INTERVIEW ROOM - 1994

INSERT CARD: CALIFORNIA CORCORAN STATE PRISON, 1994

The image is grainy, flickering at the edges like an old VHS cassette left too long in the sun. A digital time code crawls along the bottom of the screen—disjointed, occasionally stalling.

The audio buzzes with reverb, like a voice echoing inside a long-forgotten metal tank. There's a faint hum of fluorescent lighting overhead, constant and oppressive.

Charles Manson, age 60, sits shackled and cuffed to a hard wooden chair in the center of the frame. His long, stringy gray hair hangs down over his face, barely hiding the glint in his sunken eyes. A scruffy mustache and goatee give him the look of a prophet gone to seed.

Behind him, slightly blurred in the depth of field, two stoic prison guards stand against the concrete wall, arms crossed. They're out of focus—almost spectral.

Manson shifts in his seat, his posture coiled like a rattlesnake resting in the dust. He leans slightly forward, eyes fixed on someone off-camera—a faceless interviewer, silent and unseen.

                    CHARLES
               (voice soft, hypnotic)
          It's very difficult... to explain
          ten or fifteen years in two or
          three minutes.

His fingers tap lightly against the arm of the chair, the cuffs clinking faintly.

                    CHARLES (CONT'D)
          The reality of words... only say
          so much. The reality of
          motion—that moves in prison—It
          moves on life and death.
                    (MORE)

                    CHARLES (CONT'D)
              (beat)
          On what they call the main line.

His tone shifts, more grounded now. His eyes narrow.

                    CHARLES (CONT'D)
          That reality comes from handball
          courts, from weight liftin' piles,
          from someone dropping weight on
          somebody else's head... from
          somebody owing something of a blood
          family debt...

He trails off briefly, letting the silence simmer.

                    CHARLES (CONT'D)
          The way it burns back and forth...
              (pauses, reflective)
          So, if Watson has got something he
          can't face— I go face his death for
          him... Then he owes me back.

He leans closer to the camera, voice low and sharp now.

                    CHARLES (CONT'D)
          Then the Frenchman takes his spoils
          And goes off into the battle for
          me— Now I owe him one heart.

He flashes a crooked smile.

                    CHARLES (CONT'D)
          So I come back to Watson... And I
          say: You pay the Frenchman what you
          owe me.

He tilts his head like a preacher delivering hard gospel.

                    CHARLES (CONT'D)
          He says: "How do I pay it?" I
          say: Don't ask me how. I'm not
          your father. Do what you're told.
          Pay your debt or get off my road.

A moment of silence.

Then—

                    CHARLES (CONT'D)
          So he pays what he has to pay.
          Does what he has to do. I didn't
          direct him to do anything. I told
          him to be a man. Stand up for
          himself.

Manson rocks slightly in his chair, his eyes locked on the
off-camera presence, expression intense and unblinking.

                    CHARLES (CONT'D)
          I didn't tell him what he should
          do, or how he should do whatever he
          had to do.
                    (beat)
          I said he has to do... what he has
          to do.

Another long pause. The fluorescent lights buzz louder.

                    CHARLES (CONT'D)
          Wilson knows that. Claiborne knows
          that. The street knows that. The
          penitentiary knows that. The
          brotherhood knows that.

Manson slouches back slightly. A crooked smirk plays across
his lips—calculated, cold.

He doesn't blink.

The camera holds on him.

Still.

Haunted.

END FLASHBACK.

EXT. SPAHN RANCH - PRE-DAWN - AUGUST 16, 1969

The night sky is deep violet, fading slowly to a pale gray on
the horizon. Spahn Ranch, nestled in the rocky hills of
Chatsworth, lies silent beneath the sleeping moon. The dusty
movie set, once home to aging cowboys and horses, is now a
haven for long-haired youth, scattered in trailers, shacks,
and bunkhouses.

It is deceptively peaceful—eerily so.

EXT. SPAHN RANCH - PERIMETER - SAME TIME

A caravan of dark vehicles—vans, trucks, patrol cars—descends
like a phantom army, headlights off, engines low. Over one
hundred officers from the Special Enforcement Detail (L.A.
County Sheriff's elite SWAT team) take position.

They move with military precision, fanning out through the
dry brush and boulders that surround the ranch.

Armed with M1 carbines, pump shotguns, revolvers, and bullhorns, they coordinate silently, each man knowing exactly where to strike.

INT. SHACKS AND TRAILERS - CONTINUOUS

Inside the makeshift homes, members of the Manson Family sleep, sprawled across dirty mattresses, tangled together like vines—some under the influence, others in deep unconsciousness.

Tex Watson snores softly beneath a threadbare blanket. Lynette "Squeaky" Fromme stirs, sensing something.

Susan Atkins lies half-awake, eyes open but unfocused.

EXT. SPAHN RANCH - COMMAND POST - SAME TIME

A commanding officer raises a flare gun.

                    COMMANDER
               (into radio)
          On my mark.

He fires.

A bright RED FLARE streaks into the sky, arcing above the ranch like a signal from war.

EXT. SPAHN RANCH - MOMENTS LATER

ALL HELL BREAKS LOOSE.

Loudspeakers blare:

                    LOUDSPEAKER (O.S.)
          SHERIFF'S DEPARTMENT! EVERYBODY
          FREEZE! HANDS IN THE AIR!

BOOM! The sound of doors kicked in.

CRASH! A window shatters.

Men in black tactical gear storm the buildings, rifles at the ready, flashlights slicing through the darkness.

WOMEN SCREAM.

DOGS BARK.

BEDS FLIP.

CHAOS UNLEASHED.

INT. MAIN BUNKHOUSE - MOMENTS LATER

Charles Manson, groggy but composed, sits cross-legged on the
floor as officers swarm inside.

                    DEPUTY
                 (yelling)
          Down on your face! Now!

Manson lifts his hands slowly, grinning faintly beneath
tangled hair and beard.

                    CHARLES
          What took you so long?

They force him down, cuffing him behind his back.

EXT. RANCH YARD - CONTINUOUS

The Family members are lined up one by one, handcuffed,
dazed. Some cry. Some sneer. Others just stand silent,
waiting for what comes next.

A deputy opens the door to a shed, revealing a half-assembled
dune buggy surrounded by Volkswagen parts.

                    DEPUTY
                 (into radio)
          Got another one. Looks like it's
          from a chop shop.

They haul out more stolen engines, stripped chassis, and
forged registration plates—evidence of an elaborate auto
theft ring Manson's followers had been operating under the
radar.

EXT. DIRT ROAD LEAVING THE RANCH - LATER

Paddy wagons roll out of Spahn Ranch, filled with 26 arrested
Family members, including Manson. The sun is rising over the
hills, casting light on a scene of total devastation.

From the back of the last wagon, Manson watches the ranch
shrink behind him—his sanctuary now overrun.

INT. SHERIFF'S STATION - DAYS LATER

A television plays the evening news:

                         ANCHOR (V.O.)
            In a dramatic raid this weekend,
            Sheriff's deputies detained over
            two dozen residents of Spahn Ranch,
            believed to be involved in a stolen
            vehicle operation. Charges were
            dropped Tuesday due to a technical
            error in the warrants.

INT. LOS ANGELES COUNTY COURTHOUSE - COURTROOM - DAY

BANG. A gavel slams, echoing through the chamber.

The prisoners are released.

Manson walks out of the holding area, smiling again. Not
because he's free—but because he knows they still don't know
what they're really dealing with.

INSERT CARD: JUST SEVEN DAYS LATER, THE BODIES OF LENO AND
ROSEMARY LABIANCA WOULD BE DISCOVERED.

EXT. SPAHN MOVIE RANCH - LATE AUGUST 1969 - DUSK

The sun sets low over Spahn Ranch, casting long shadows
across the broken-down Western movie set. Horses graze
quietly in the dust. A radio crackles from inside the main
house, echoing news of the Tate-LaBianca murders—but no one
at the ranch says a word.

                    RADIO ANNOUNCER (V.O.)
            —police have confirmed the identity
            of the victims at 10050 Cielo
            Drive, including actress Sharon
            Tate—

The Family sits in silence. Eyes shift. Breath held.

                    RADIO ANNOUNCER (V.O.) (CON'T)
            —and this morning, two more bodies
            found in Los Feliz...

Manson, sitting alone at a weathered picnic table, sharpening
a knife, stares across the dusty lot at a distant
figure—DONALD "SHORTY" SHEA, a rugged 35-year-old stuntman
and ranch hand, talking to one of the wranglers near the
stables.

Shorty had always been wary of Manson and his growing group
of followers. He made no secret of his disdain for them.

And now, after the August 16 SWAT raid that led to Manson's temporary arrest and the brief collapse of their sanctuary, Manson's paranoia is boiling over.

INT. MAIN HOUSE - NIGHT

A handful of Family members—BRUCE DAVIS, male white, 27, Tex Watson, Steve "Clem" Grogan, and Charles Manson—sit in a circle on the floor, surrounded by candlelight, pot smoke, and the droning echo of Revolution 9 spinning on a battered turntable.

Manson stares into the flame of a candle. His voice is low, controlled, and ominous.

                    CHARLES
          Somebody brought the heat down on
          us.

No one answers. Tension rises like smoke in the air.

                    CHARLES (CONT'D)
          Somebody whispered to the pigs.
          Somebody's a rat. A snitch.
               (beat)
          And I think we know who.

He lifts his eyes. All heads slowly turn toward the door—toward the image in their minds of Shorty.

                    BRUCE DAVIS
               (quietly)
          You think it was him? Shorty?

Manson doesn't blink.

                    CHARLES
          I don't think anything. I know.
          He was never with us. He's been
          fighting us since day one. Now
          he's trying to take us out from the
          inside.
               (beat)
          He brought the raid. He called the
          cops.

                    STEVE "CLEM" GROGAN
          He's been talking about us. Said
          we were freaks. Said he was gonna
          get George Spahn to kick us out.

                         CHARLES
                    (nods)
               He's got poison in his mouth. That
               poison spreads.

He looks at Bruce Davis directly.

                         CHARLES (CONT'D)
               I need you to handle it. Quiet.
               Clean.

                         BRUCE DAVIS
                    (soft, conflicted)
               You want him... gone?

Manson doesn't flinch. His smile is thin, cruel.

                         CHARLES
               He's already gone. He just doesn't
               know it yet.

EXT. SPAHN RANCH - NEXT MORNING

Shorty walks across the ranch yard, wiping grease from his
hands. He's been working on one of the ranch trucks. He
nods politely at a group of Family members sitting near a
fire—but they say nothing.

He senses it now. He's being watched. The usual chill in
the air has grown cold.

INT. FAMILY MEETING ROOM - LATER

Bruce Davis sits alone with Tex Watson, both quiet.

                         BRUCE DAVIS
               Charlie says he's a snitch. That
               he deserves what's coming.

Tex leans in, whispering like a priest confessing to another.

                         TEX WATSON
               I don't even think it matters
               anymore. If Charlie says he's
               out... he's out.

EXT. SPAHN RANCH - EARLY MORNING - AUGUST 26, 1969

A thick haze hangs over the dusty expanse of Spahn Ranch.
The sun has just started to crest the canyon ridge.

Donald "Shorty" Shea, rugged and grizzled, wipes grease from his hands. He squints toward the barn as Susan Atkins approaches, her tone unusually sweet.

                    SUSAN ATKINS
                (smiling)
          Hey Shorty... Charlie wants you to
          check something out down by the
          parts yard.

Shorty hesitates, sensing something off. Still, he nods and follows. His boots crunch against the dry earth.

EXT. RANCH ROAD - MOMENTS LATER

A battered Ford sedan waits near the horse stables. The doors are open. Behind the wheel is Steve "Clem" Grogan, fidgeting with a wrench on his lap. Bruce Davis stands beside the car, eyes locked on the horizon.

Charles "Tex" Watson leans against the passenger door, silent. Manson stands nearby, arms folded, watching it all—calculating.

                    CHARLES
                (to Shorty)
          We need to make a run down to the
          old yard. You coming?

Shorty nods slowly. He glances at the group, then at Susan, then back to the car.

                    SHORTY SHEA
                (gruff)
          Yeah... alright.

He climbs into the front passenger seat. Davis and Grogan slide into the back.

EXT. RANCH HILLSIDE - LATER

The car winds along a narrow dirt path behind the ranch. Dust kicks up behind the tires as they descend toward a secluded ravine.

Grogan grips the pipe wrench tighter, knuckles white.

Suddenly—

THWACK.

The wrench comes down hard on Shorty's head. He jerks
forward with a shout of pain, stunned.

                    SHORTY SHEA
                  (crying out)
            What the hell—!

Before he can react, Watson lunges across the seat, a blade
flashing in the light. A brutal struggle erupts inside the
vehicle.

Shorty flails, bloodied but still fighting. He kicks the
door open and stumbles out into the dirt.

EXT. BOTTOM OF THE HILL - MINUTES LATER

They drag Shorty, semi-conscious and groaning, down into the
ravine. His shirt is soaked red. His breathing is shallow.

Davis looks away. Grogan stares blankly.

Watson kneels beside him.

                    TEX
                  (quietly)
            You brought the pigs here. Charlie
            said you talked.

Shorty tries to speak, but only gurgles escape.

Watson raises the blade again.

The sun is high now. The silence in the canyon is pierced
only by the sound of buzzards circling overhead.

EXT. RANCH - HOURS LATER

Back at Spahn Ranch, Manson sits alone, strumming a guitar.

He doesn't ask what happened.

He already knows.

INSERT CARD: SHORTY SHEA'S BODY WAS NOT DISCOVERED UNTIL
1977. SEVERAL MANSON FAMILY MEMBERS LATER CONFESSED TO THE
MURDER AND WERE CONVICTED.

EXT. SUBURBAN STREET - SHERMAN OAKS, CALIFORNIA - SEPTEMBER
1, 1969 - LATE MORNING

The streets of Sherman Oaks are quiet, sun-drenched, and
neatly trimmed. Lawns are mowed, sprinklers tick across
sidewalks, and children's bicycles rest against picket
fences.

A ten-year-old boy, TOMMY, in a striped T-shirt and dusty
sneakers, kicks a rock down the sidewalk near his house. He
pauses beside a row of overgrown bushes separating two homes,
curious as a glint catches his eye.

He crouches down, brushing back the branches—And freezes.

Beneath the shrub lies a .22 caliber Longhorn revolver, half-
covered in dry leaves and dirt. Its long barrel reflects the
light, dull but unmistakably metallic.

                    TOMMY
               (confused, calling out)
          Mom! Dad!

INT. LIVING ROOM - TOMMY'S HOUSE - MOMENTS LATER

Tommy's parents, MARTHA and RICHARD, rush out the front door
as Tommy leads them back to the spot.

                    RICHARD
               (frowning)
          That's a real gun...

He leans down, carefully examining it without touching. The
serial number is visible but partially obscured with grime.

                    MARTHA
               (concerned)
          We need to call the police. Now.

EXT. SHERMAN OAKS RESIDENTIAL STREET - 30 MINUTES LATER

A black-and-white LAPD cruiser pulls up. Two officers step
out, casual but alert. One wears sunglasses and takes a
notepad from his breast pocket.

                    OFFICER #1
          Where is it?

Tommy points silently. His eyes are wide with excitement and
unease.

The officer kneels, lifts the revolver with a pencil through the trigger guard, and slips it into an evidence bag.

                    OFFICER #2
          Might be stolen. Could've been
          tossed by some junkie.

They thank the family, take down their names, and assure them it'll be checked in at the lab.

INT. LAPD PROPERTY ROOM - LATER THAT DAY

The revolver is logged, tagged, and placed on a shelf among dozens of other unclaimed or unlinked weapons. No rush. No urgency.

There's no connection made between the .22 caliber revolver found in Sherman Oaks...

...and the massacre at Cielo Drive three weeks earlier.

OVER BLACK: THIS REVOLVER WAS LATER CONFIRMED TO BE THE WEAPON USED BY CHARLES "TEX" WATSON IN THE TATE MURDERS. AT THE TIME, IT SAT UNCONNECTED IN LAPD EVIDENCE STORAGE.

EXT. BARKER RANCH - PANAMINT MOUNTAINS, CALIFORNIA - OCTOBER 12, 1969 - PRE-DAWN

The jagged cliffs of the Panamint Range rise like prehistoric bones out of the desert floor. A full moon casts ghostly shadows over the abandoned mining property known as Barker Ranch, deep in the heart of Death Valley's remote wilderness.

The silence is broken by the low rumble of Inyo County Sheriff's vehicles crawling across the dirt trail, headlights off, guided only by moonlight and memory.

Inside the lead Jeep, Sheriff Don Ward scans the darkness, his face set with quiet determination. He holds a hand-drawn map and a mug of lukewarm coffee.

They're not here for murder—they're after suspects in an arson investigation and a stolen vehicle ring. But what they find will be far more chilling.

EXT. BARKER RANCH CABIN - DAWN

The compound comes into view: a collection of crude structures nestled against red rock and scraggly desert brush.

A rusted school bus, now home to several runaways, is parked crooked near a shack. An old stone cabin, smoke curling from its chimney, anchors the center.

Suddenly—

LOUDSPEAKER BLARES: "SHERIFF'S DEPARTMENT! COME OUT WITH YOUR HANDS UP!"

Chaos erupts.

Figures scramble from inside, some barefoot, half-dressed. Dogs bark. Someone screams. A naked man bolts into the brush before being tackled by a deputy.

INT. BARKER RANCH CABIN - MINUTES LATER

Deputies burst inside. Smoke from the fireplace thickens the air. The room is a tangle of filthy blankets, candles, and hand-drawn symbols on the walls. Wide-eyed women with dreadlocked hair crouch together. Some laugh. Some cry.

Susan Atkins, wild-haired and glassy-eyed, raises her hands slowly. She smiles faintly as if greeting old friends.

                    SUSAN ATKINS
          You're too late, pigs. We already
          know how this ends.

She's cuffed and led out.

INT. BACK ROOM - CONTINUOUS

A deputy inspects the tiny kitchen, opening cupboards and poking behind shelves. He nearly misses it—a set of worn cabinet doors under the sink, half-concealed behind a hanging burlap curtain.

He yanks the curtain aside and opens the doors.

Inside:

Charles Manson curls into the fetal position, wedged tightly into the cabinet, dressed in filthy buckskins, eyes gleaming from the darkness. For a beat, he says nothing.

Then—

                    CHARLES
               (calmly)
          How now, brown cow?

The deputy jerks back, stunned.

                    CHARLES (CONT'D)
          You're not looking for me. But
          here I am.

He slowly unfolds himself from the cabinet like a spider from
its web, hands raised, posture regal despite the grime. He's
calm, collected, and almost amused.

EXT. BARKER RANCH - LATER

Twenty-four people are loaded into vans and Jeeps. Manson
walks barefoot, flanked by deputies. His face is unreadable.

He isn't yet the face of evil.

Not yet the name on every front page.

But the clock is ticking.

INSERT CARD: CHARLES MANSON WAS BOOKED FOR ARSON AND GRAND
THEFT. WITHIN WEEKS, HE WOULD BE NAMED THE ORCHESTRATOR OF
THE MOST INFAMOUS MASS MURDERS IN AMERICAN HISTORY.

INT. DORMITORY 8000 - LOS ANGELES COUNTY WOMEN'S JAIL - NIGHT
- NOVEMBER 6, 1969

Flickering fluorescent lights buzz overhead in the large,
echo-filled dormitory. Rows of metal-framed bunk beds line
the walls. The concrete floor is cold, even through the
issued slippers. A TV plays faintly in the corner—some late-
night sitcom drowned out by murmuring voices and the
occasional cough.

Susan Atkins, lean and wiry, sits cross-legged on her bunk,
smiling vaguely to herself as she braids strands of her hair.
Her eyes are wild but serene, faraway. She hums a tune that
no one else recognizes—something dissonant, minor, hypnotic.

On the bunk beside her, VIRGINIA GRAHAM, 35, an older, sharp-
tongued inmate with a keen instinct for survival, eyes Atkins
warily. She lights a cigarette and watches.

                    VIRGINIA GRAHAM
               (low, curious)
          You're in for something big, huh?

Atkins turns her head slowly, almost as if she's been waiting
to be asked.

                    SUSAN ATKINS
               (smiling, dreamy)
          You ever hear of a man named
          Charlie?

Graham raises an eyebrow.

                    VIRGINIA
          Charles Manson?

                    SUSAN ATKINS
               (singsong)
          A beautiful cat. A man who knows
          the truth about the world... and
          how it's all comin' down.

She leans in slightly, her voice dropping to a whisper.

                    SUSAN ATKINS (CONT'D)
          I was there. At the house. With
          Sharon Tate.

Graham freezes mid-puff.

                    VIRGINIA
          What house?

Atkins tilts her head, eyes alight like a child telling a
fairytale.

                    SUSAN ATKINS
          Cielo Drive. We went there to do
          Charlie's work. I found her in
          bed... wearin' just her little
          bikini bra and panties. She begged
          me to let her live... so her baby
          could live.

                    VIRGINIA
               (flat)
          You let her go?

                    SUSAN ATKINS
               (gleeful)
          No. I held her down while Tex did
          his thing. Then I stabbed her too.
          I tasted her blood. It was warm.

Virginia stares at her in horror, unable to mask the
revulsion.

                    SUSAN ATKINS (CONT'D)
          Charlie says it's just meat. Just
          bodies. No souls.

Graham backs away slightly, but Atkins isn't finished. She
giggles, as if telling a secret.

                    SUSAN ATKINS (CONT'D)
          There's a list, you know. Big
          names.

                    VIRGINIA
          What kind of list?

                    SUSAN
          People we were gonna take out next.
          Charlie's plan. Gotta start the
          war. Elizabeth Taylor, Richard
          Burton, Steve McQueen, Tom Jones...
                    (she counts on her
                     fingers)
          Frank Sinatra—we were gonna cut him
          up and hang his guts on a
          chandelier.

Graham can't hide her disbelief.

                    VIRGINIA
          Jesus Christ...

                    SUSAN
                    (smiling proudly)
          Helter Skelter, baby. It's comin'.

INT. COMMON AREA - NEXT DAY

Virginia Graham paces nervously, whispering to another
inmate, RONNIE HOWARD, male white, 30s, a friend of hers with
connections to the outside.

                    VIRGINIA
          She told me everything. Tate. The
          baby. The others. Names, dates...
          Jesus, she was proud of it.

Ronnie stares at her, stunned.

                    RONNIE
          You've gotta tell someone.

INT. LAPD HEADQUARTERS - DAYS LATER

A detective drops a thick manila folder on a desk. Inside: a
report taken from a tip passed through Ronnie Howard, via
Graham.

The words written in block letters: "Inmate Susan Atkins may
be involved in Tate murders."

A stunned silence falls over the room.

                    DETECTIVE #1
          Get the DA.

INSERT CARD: THIS TIP WOULD LEAD TO A FORMAL INTERVIEW WITH
SUSAN ATKINS AND THE ARREST OF CHARLES MANSON AND OTHER
MEMBERS OF THE FAMILY FOR THE TATE-LABIANCA MURDERS.

INT. LOS ANGELES POLICE HEADQUARTERS - HOMICIDE INTERVIEW
ROOM - NOVEMBER 12, 1969 - AFTERNOON

The walls are bare, the lighting cold and direct. A tape
recorder sits at the center of a scratched metal table. Two
LAPD homicide detectives—Detective Sergeant MICHAEL McMGANN,
male white, 40, and Detective PHILIP SARTUCHI, male white,
38,—sit across from a broad-shouldered man with a long beard,
leather vest, and patches.

AL SPRINGER, early 30s, is a member of the Straight Satans
motorcycle gang—a tight-lipped, distrustful type who speaks
when he wants to, and only if you've earned it.

He lights a cigarette with calloused hands and leans back in
his chair.

                    DETECTIVE SARTUCHI
                 (starting the tape
                  recorder)
          November 12. Interview with Al
          Springer, in relation to the
          LaBianca homicide case.

                    DETECTIVE MCGANN
          Appreciate you coming in, Al. We
          heard through the grapevine your
          club may have crossed paths with a
          guy named Charles Manson.

Springer exhales slowly. Smirks.

                    SPRINGER
          Yeah. Charlie.
             (beat)
          Crazy little bastard out at Spahn
          Ranch.

                    DETECTIVE MCGANN
          You met him?

                    SPRINGER
          Couple times. August maybe. Came
          sniffin' around like he wanted to
          make friends. Wanted the club's
          protection, if I remember right.

               DETECTIVE SARTUCHI
          Protection from what?

                    SPRINGER
          Didn't say. But he had this way of
          talking—like everything was cosmic
          and all roads led back to him.
          Offered me my pick of, what,
          eighteen girls he had out there.
          No joke—they were all over the
          place. Naked. Trippin'. Callin'
          him "God." It was a circus.

               DETECTIVE MCGANN
          You said he mentioned something
          about... knocking people off?

Springer shifts, flicks ash onto the floor.

                    SPRINGER
          Yeah. After a couple beers he got
          loose. Said they'd gone out and
          "knocked off five piggies." His
          words. "Piggies." Laughed about
          it. Said it was "necessary for the
          revolution."

               DETECTIVE SARTUCHI
          He say who?

                    SPRINGER
          Not names, no. But he said they'd
          made it "loud and clear." That
          they "left a message." Then he
          said something that stuck with me.
               (beat)
          He said they wrote "something about
          pigs" in blood. On a fridge.

The room goes still.

               DETECTIVE MCGANN
               (incredulous)
          The refrigerator?

                         SPRINGER
               Yeah. Said it real proud-like.
               "Wrote on the fridge in blood."
               Thought it was funny.

The detectives exchange glances. Until now, only the
killers—and the investigators—knew that "Healter Skelter" and
"Death to Pigs" had been written in blood at the LaBianca
house.

                         DETECTIVE SARTUCHI
               That wasn't public knowledge.

                         DETECTIVE MCGANN
               Are you absolutely sure he said
               that?

                         SPRINGER
               Word for word. Thought he was a
               bullshitter. I mean, who confesses
               that kinda thing to someone they
               barely know?

Springer leans forward, tone suddenly serious.

                         SPRINGER (CONT'D)
               But now I'm not so sure he was
               bullshitting.

INT. HOMICIDE SQUAD ROOM - MOMENTS LATER

The detectives step into the hallway, close the door behind
them. Both men are now visibly energized—haunted.

                         DETECTIVE SARTUCHI
               First the girl in jail... now this
               biker.

                         DETECTIVE MCGANN
               Different circles. Same story.

They don't say the name. They don't have to. It's becoming
clear: Charles Manson isn't just a desert weirdo. He's the
key.

INSERT CARD: AL SPRINGER'S STATEMENT WAS LATER USED TO
CORROBORATE SUSAN ATKINS' CONFESSION. IT MARKED THE FIRST
TIME SOMEONE OUTSIDE THE FAMILY HAD DIRECTLY TIED MANSON TO
THE TATE-LABIANCA KILLINGS.

INT. LOS ANGELES POLICE DEPARTMENT - HOMICIDE DIVISION -
NOVEMBER 17, 1969 - EVENING

Fluorescent lights buzz above worn desks piled with manila
folders and photographs of carnage. Detectives move like
ghosts, exhausted but driven.

DANNY DECARLO, male Caucasian, 27, lean and tough-looking,
sits across from Detectives McGann and Sartuchi, arms folded
across his patched biker jacket. A member of the Straight
Satans motorcycle club, DeCarlo had lived at Spahn Ranch for
months and knew the Family inside and out.

He lights a cigarette, hands shaking slightly.

                    DECARLO
          You wanna know who you're lookin'
          for? It's Manson. Charlie Manson.

The detectives lean forward.

                    DETECTIVE SARTUCHI
          Why now, Danny? Why are you
          talking?

                    DECARLO
          Because I heard one of 'em—don't
          know which—say "we got five
          piggies." Just like that.
          Laughin'. After Cielo. And
          Charlie... he asked me once what
          you use to decompose a body.

                    DETECTIVE MCGANN
          He asked you that?

                    DECARLO
          Yeah. Said he might need it
          "someday." I thought it was just
          more crazy Charlie talk... but
          then I saw the blood writing on TV.

He ashes the cigarette in a Styrofoam cup.

                    DECARLO (CONT'D)
          It ain't just acid and hippie
          nonsense. It's murder. Lots of
          it.

INT. LOS ANGELES DISTRICT ATTORNEY'S OFFICE - NOVEMBER 18, 1969 - MORNING

A hushed tension fills the room as top brass from the L.A. County District Attorney's office review what's now known about the Tate-LaBianca killings. Names are listed on a whiteboard. "CHARLES MANSON" is circled in red.

E. PAUL FITZGERALD, male white, 50, the supervising D.A., turns to a man at the end of the conference table—VINCENT BUGLIOSI, early 30s, sharp-suited, intense eyes.

> FITZGERALD
> Vincent, we need a prosecutor who
> can handle a circus. And still
> bring home a conviction. This
> one... this one's going to be
> watched around the world.

Bugliosi nods, already assembling arguments in his mind.

> BUGLIOSI
> Then we better get started today.

EXT. SPAHN MOVIE RANCH - NOVEMBER 19, 1969 - DAY

A search team of LAPD officers, Vincent Bugliosi, and detectives trek across the dusty, windblown ruins of Spahn Ranch. The stables are crumbling. Burned-out cars litter the lot.

They move into the canyon behind the ranch, following DeCarlo's tip.

BANG.

One officer hits metal—then uncovers a rusted tin can filled with .22 caliber bullets and spent shell casings. Nearby: a scorched makeshift target tacked to a boulder, riddled with holes.

> BUGLIOSI
> These are the same rounds used at
> Cielo Drive.

> DETECTIVE MCGANN
> We might've just tied them to the
> scene.

Bugliosi kneels, eyes focused—this isn't just murder anymore. It's premeditated, methodical. It's a doctrine of violence.

EXT. BARKER RANCH - DEATH VALLEY - NOVEMBER 20, 1969 - MIDDAY

A convoy of Jeeps winds through sun-scorched rock formations, arriving at the isolation of Barker Ranch.

The search team dismounts, fanning out across the desolate compound. Bugliosi follows behind a deputy into the main cabin, now abandoned and eerie, the silence nearly spiritual.

Inside, he stops at the low cabinet under the sink. A DEPUTY crouches and opens the small doors.

> DEPUTY
> This is where they pulled him out.
> Manson. Curled up like a goddamn
> gopher.

Bugliosi stares at the empty space, trying to imagine the man—the myth—stuffed into the shadows like a ghost waiting to reappear.

They move on toward the ravine.

EXT. DRY GULLY - NEAR BARKER RANCH - MOMENTS LATER

In the rusted hulk of an abandoned school bus, deputies find scattered trash, burned papers, and a stack of molded, sun-warped WWII magazines.

Bugliosi flips through one.

HEADLINE: "The Rise of Hitler"

Another: "The Fuhrer's Final Days"

He looks at the cover, then across the lifeless landscape.

> BUGLIOSI (QUIETLY)
> He wasn't just playing guru. He was
> trying to start a war.

INSERT CARD: BY LATE NOVEMBER, POLICE HAD PHYSICAL EVIDENCE, EYEWITNESS TESTIMONY, AND CONFESSIONS. WHAT REMAINED WAS THE TASK OF BUILDING THE CASE—AND BRINGING CHARLES MANSON TO JUSTICE.

INT. LOS ANGELES POLICE DEPARTMENT - HOMICIDE DIVISION -
EARLY DECEMBER 1969 - NIGHT

The atmosphere is electric with momentum. A dozen detectives
move between corkboards filled with photos, crime scene maps,
and red yarn connecting dots that span from Spahn Ranch to
Cielo Drive to Barker Ranch.

At the center: a photo of Charles Manson pinned above a list
of names. Red ink circles five.

                    DETECTIVE SARTUCHI (O.S.)
               We have them. All five.

The names echo as if carved into stone:

Susan Atkins

Patricia Krenwinkel

Leslie Van Houten

Linda Kasabian

Charles "Tex" Watson

INT. DORMITORY 8000 - LOS ANGELES COUNTY WOMEN'S JAIL - NIGHT

Susan Atkins, gaunt and dreamy-eyed, lies on her bunk humming
to herself, entirely detached from the world outside. A
CORRECTIONS OFFICER appears at the bars.

                    CORRECTIONS OFFICER
               Atkins. You're being transferred.
               Formal charges coming.

She doesn't flinch. Instead, she grins, as if she's known
this was coming all along.

                    SUSAN ATKINS
               It's all part of the plan.

She's cuffed and led out into the corridor.

INT. SHERIFF'S OFFICE - LOS ANGELES - EARLY MORNING

In a briefing room, detectives place five mug shots on the
table. A new operation is underway.

COMMANDING OFFICER
Get them. All of them. Coordinate
with local jurisdictions. No
delays, no mistakes.

EXT. DOWNTOWN LOS ANGELES - APARTMENT COMPLEX - DAY

Leslie Van Houten, dazed and soft-spoken, is escorted down
the steps of a small apartment building by two plainclothes
LAPD officers. She clutches a paperback copy of The Prophet
by Kahlil Gibran. No resistance.

INT. SHERIFF'S DEPARTMENT - COLLIN COUNTY, TEXAS - NIGHT

Charles "Tex" Watson, tall, heavy-built, sits handcuffed at a
metal desk under harsh light. The local Texas sheriff,
skeptical but cooperative, talks with LAPD over the phone.

TEX WATSON
You don't understand. Charlie's
got the answers. We were just the
instruments.

Watson had tried to lay low at his parents' house in
McKinney, Texas, but the dragnet found him. The warrant:
suspicion of murder, five counts.

INT. POLICE STATION - MOBILE, ALABAMA - NIGHT

A tired and anxious Patricia Krenwinkel, stares at the wall
in a holding cell. She was arrested at the home of her
father's relatives—1,800 miles away from Los Angeles.

She had dyed her hair. Changed her clothes. But the guilt
followed.

DETECTIVE (O.S.)
She didn't run far. Charlie never
let them.

INT. POLICE DEPARTMENT - CONCORD, NEW HAMPSHIRE - DAY

Linda Kasabian, barefoot, thin, and visibly shaken, walks
into the police station voluntarily.

She looks nothing like a murderer. More like a runaway as
she stands in front of an OFFICER.

                    LINDA KASABIAN
          I'd like to speak to someone about
          a murder in California.

                    OFFICER
          Which one?

                    LINDA
          The one with the baby.

INT. LOS ANGELES DISTRICT ATTORNEY'S OFFICE - LATER THAT WEEK

Vincent Bugliosi enters the war room, now stacked with case
files, audio tapes, and photos.

                    BUGLIOSI
          They're in custody. All of them.

He turns to the team of junior prosecutors.

                    BUGLIOSI (CONT'D)
          Now we build the case. And we make
          history.

INSERT CARD: BY MID-DECEMBER 1969, ALL FIVE OF THE CORE
TATE-LABIANCA MURDER SUSPECTS WERE IN CUSTODY. WHAT FOLLOWED
WAS ONE OF THE MOST SENSATIONAL AND SHOCKING TRIALS IN
AMERICAN HISTORY.

INT. LOS ANGELES COUNTY COURTHOUSE - SUPERIOR COURTROOM -
JANUARY 25, 1971 - DAY

The air is thick with anticipation. After nearly ten months
of shocking testimony, chilling behavior, and legal
theatrics, the jury has returned.

The 12 jurors—exhausted, pale, eyes heavy from the weight of
what they've seen—file slowly into the jury box. Their
expressions are solemn, unreadable.

Spectators, reporters, and family members of the victims lean
in. Camera shutters click in a dull rhythm from the press
gallery.

At the defense table sit:

Charles Manson, unshaven, with a small X carved into his
forehead, now darkened into a crude swastika.

Susan Atkins, thin and glassy-eyed, smiling faintly as though
none of this is real.

Patricia Krenwinkle, stiff-backed, eyes forward.

Leslie Van Houten, looking far younger than her crimes suggest—her jaw clenched, arms folded.

The CLERK rises and opens the sealed envelope. The judge nods.

> CLERK
> We, the jury, find the defendant Charles Manson... guilty of first-degree murder on all counts.

Gasps ripple through the courtroom.

> CLERK (CONT'D)
> We find the defendant Susan Atkins... guilty of first-degree murder on all counts.

> CLERK (CONT'D)
> We find the defendant Patricia Krenwinkel... guilty of first-degree murder on all counts.

> CLERK (CONT'D)
> We find the defendant Leslie Van Houten... guilty of first-degree murder.

Manson grins, suddenly rising in his seat. Bailiffs tense.

> CHARLES
> (shouting)
> You people have no authority over me!

> JUDGE OLDER
> Mr. Manson—sit down or be removed.

> PATRICIA KRENWINKEL
> (firm, shouting)
> You have judged yourselves!

> SUSAN ATKINS
> (snarling)
> Better lock your doors and watch your own kids.

> LESLIE VAN HOUTEN
> (under her breath,
> defiant)
> The whole system is a game.

Reporters scribble wildly. A few spectators sob. Others sit in stunned silence.

INT. COURTROOM - PENALTY PHASE - MARCH 29, 1971

Weeks later, the trial's final chapter.

The jury returns once more, having deliberated on the punishment. The courtroom is quieter this time. Heavier. Everyone knows what's coming.

                    CLERK
          We, the jury, fix the penalty as...
          death.

Manson stares blankly, as if already detached from his physical body.

Krenwinkel whispers a chant under her breath.

Van Houten closes her eyes.

Atkins begins to hum.

INT. COURTHOUSE HALLWAY - LATER THAT DAY

Prosecutor Vincent Bugliosi, flanked by reporters, gives a short, solemn statement:

                    BUGLIOSI
          Justice has been served, but this
          is not a victory. There is no
          victory when lives are lost on this
          scale—on both sides of the aisle.

                    NARRATION (V.O.)
          At over nine months, the Manson
          trial became the longest and most
          expensive in American history at
          the time. It was a cultural
          reckoning, a media spectacle, and a
          portrait of evil that stunned the
          world.

INSERT CARD: IN 1972, THE CALIFORNIA SUPREME COURT ABOLISHED THE DEATH PENALTY, AND THE SENTENCES FOR MANSON, ATKINS, KRENWINKEL, AND VAN HOUTEN WERE COMMUTED TO LIFE IMPRISONMENT.

FLASHBACK:

INT. CALIFORNIA CORCORAN STATE PRISON - INTERVIEW ROOM - 1994
- NIGHT

INSERT CARD: California State Prison, Corcoran - November 12,
1994

The image is grainy, degraded like a worn VHS tape. A faint
timecode ticks away in the bottom corner. The audio hums
with reverb, the voices slightly warped—raw, unsettling.

The room is sterile, lit by a harsh overhead fluorescent bulb
that buzzes softly. A wooden chair, bolted to the floor,
sits center-frame. Seated in it is Charles Manson, age 60,
shackled at the waist and wrists. His beige prison jumpsuit
sags on his wiry frame. His hair is long, matted, wild
around his shoulders. A swastika tattoo scars the middle of
his forehead.

Behind him, two unmoving guards, out of focus, stand like
statues by the cinderblock wall. They're silent. Watching.

Manson stares forward, breathing steadily, his expression
fixed in a tense scowl.

He shifts in his seat, restraining himself—barely.

> CHARLES
> (gritting his teeth)
> I never directed traffic on no, no
> street corner about anything,
> man...
> (pause)
> I haven't got time for that.

He leans forward slightly. The chain clinks as he tugs at
the waist restraint.

An inaudible question is asked off-camera—a man's voice,
distorted, buried beneath the hiss of analog tape.

Manson squints toward the interviewer, his eyes flashing,
full of contempt and fury. He answers in clipped bursts.

> CHARLES (CONT'D)
> I'm not gonna get involved.
> (beat)
> I'm not that... what... insane?

He laughs once, dark and bitter.

> CHARLES (CONT'D)
> You know I'm crazy.
> (smiles briefly)
> But I'm not you, you know?

He gestures with his cuffed hands, his tone building in speed and volume.

> CHARLES (CONT'D)
> I mean, I can—I can play that game.
> But I—you know, I'm not gonna take
> a chance...
> > (beat)
> ...puttin' myself back in jail—for
> what?

He leans back, exasperated. Then he points at the camera, voice rising.

> CHARLES (CONT'D)
> You deal me the hand, man! I got
> to play it! You give me the cards!

His voice deepens, almost mocking.

> CHARLES (CONT'D)
> I'm a mass murderer. I'm a hippie
> cult leader... That's the story,
> right?
> > (beat, sneering)
> So the DA gets to bring in the
> mafia from New York... and Rambo
> gets to be in the movies!

His eyes burn now—ranting, barely tethered to coherence.

> CHARLES (CONT'D)
> You see what I'm sayin'? In other
> words... Helter Skelter? That's
> just one little foot he's playin'.
> And then he comes back—comes back
> to me from Geneva...
> > (cynical grin)
> ...wants to be my sunshine—if I'll
> agree with him on his Helter
> Skelter theory.

Manson's tone drops to a low growl.

> MANSON
> I didn't have any Helter Skelter in
> my mind.
> > (beat. Then—)
> None.

He leans forward, intense and still. His breathing slows. A dark silence stretches.

Then—his mouth curls into a slow, wicked grin. His eyes
narrow, piercing.

But he says nothing else.

The hum of the tape continues for a few seconds longer.

END FLASHBACK.

                                        FADE OUT.

The End.